HUNGRY GODS

Hungry Gods is **Richa Lakhera's** third novel, she has previously written *Item Girl*, a crime novel and *Garbage Beat*, a satire on the Indian entertainment industry. A libertarian addicted to absurdism, she works as Deputy Editor at NDTV. She has a Master's in Organic Chemistry and Biotechnology and is the recipient of the Indian Council for UN Relations (ICUNR) Award for Excellence in Journalism. Richa divides her time between New Delhi and Mumbai, and is currently working on her next crime fiction novel.

Richa can be tweeted to at @RICHA_LAKHERA, and her literary agent at @SiyahiJaipur.

HUNGRY GODS

**DRUGS. SEX CULTS.
A HORRIFIC CRIME. AN UNTHINKABLE REVENGE**

RICHA LAKHERA

RUPA

Published by
Rupa Publications India Pvt. Ltd 2018
7/16, Ansari Road, Daryaganj
New Delhi 110002

Sales centres:
Allahabad Bengaluru Chennai
Hyderabad Jaipur Kathmandu
Kolkata Mumbai

Copyright © Richa Lakhera 2018

This is a work of fiction. Names, characters,
places and incidents are either the product of the author's
imagination or are used fictitiously and any resemblance to any actual person,
living or dead, events or locales is entirely coincidental

All rights reserved.
No part of this publication may be reproduced, transmitted, or stored in a retrieval
system, in any form or by any means, electronic, mechanical, photocopying, recording
or otherwise, without the prior permission of the publisher.

ISBN: 978-93-5304-079-6

First impression 2018

10 9 8 7 6 5 4 3 2 1

The moral right of the author has been asserted.

Printed by HT Media Ltd, Gr. Noida

This book is sold subject to the condition that it shall not,
by way of trade or otherwise, be lent, resold, hired out, or otherwise circulated,
without the publisher's prior consent, in any form of binding or cover
other than that in which it is published.

'But I wonder if what I will get in the end would be nothing more than a juke joint brand version of immortality.'

—Neville Valentine, the superstar

1993

She resembled a smashed tomato. When I first heard her screams from across the Dune I did not know it was going to be the day I would watch my mother's murder. She was on a low cot, a black patch of cement and mud in the factory warehouse. Her head bashed against the bed railing, limbs broken, surrounded by a restless circle of men waiting to crumple her.

'Sly witch, you suck like a dead fish—dirty dead fish.'

'Open your mouth and lick and if I as much as feel your teeth, I will slit your throat.' Panting hard like a dog, the man wouldn't stop bayoneting her face with his stick.

'Old witch is slicker than a mud pig.'

She saw me then and that punched the light debris off her eyes. We both knew she was gone too far. That even if she survived she would never live again. Her screams wouldn't stop filling the room. The man raping her used his fingers to gag her before forcing her mouth back onto his erect penis. That was the last time I saw my mother alive.

One of the men pointed at me and threw a stick. Blood rushed up my throat and I ran like the devil was after me.

A billion serrated branches, fenced off flint, tyre tracks, water reflecting pieces of black sky fell rapidly from the feet. From miles above, my soul watched my body clamber across fields of undersown stubble, fall into nettly ditches, claw out of collapsed thatches. The pressure on my chest was a beast pushing ash down my throat but I ran till the sun petered out of focus and bats flitting in the darkness gathered in the forest. She was irrevocably lost. Gone, gone. Her smells, her sight, her taste, her flesh and bones. Gone. She would never wrinkle her lovely brow in concentration nor would she ever mix her medicines with fingers bleached by non-stop work. Her sweet smells of healing sulphurs, phosphorus, and lime were all gone. She would never whisper to me about the healing spirits—some good, some really bad. She would never show me the pollen from flowers of multiple fragrances to get demented souls back from the brink, nor warn me of the blue fruit seeds which made peaceful men violent nor bring to light the stamens which healed lust at high moon. Mother paid the price for knowing too much, just like Buddhi, my best friend. I thought of all that as I ran in crazed despair along the bank of the red river. But mostly I thought of Hiri. Her flower face framed with thickly plaited ebonite coils swam before my eyes and all I wanted was to crush the life out of her for her betrayal. The strange noise from the inky darkness filled me with panic. I looked about for a place to hide in. I found a cavity big enough for a small person to fit in. The inside was dark and smelled of dead bodies, but I crawled deep into the sodden stench, summoning all my strength to hide from my hunters.

1

Dinesh Thackray
Monday, 25 October
Dinesh Thackray's studio cum office

It is hot. Hot enough to make the leaves inverted, brittle with heat, their edges furred with steam. So hot that the sky looks like a playground of creatures from an inferno bottom. Dinesh Thackray wants to take out his flesh and sit in his bones.

A man pulls up outside Thackray's bungalow and parks his motorcycle behind a large hedge with leaves resembling crumbled keratin. He slings a bulky bag across his chest and heads toward the back gate of Dinesh Thackray's office. The man is probably aware that he is being filmed, knows the position of the cameras and yet the hardness of his silent step is not unlike a killer slowly but surely gaining on its prey. Thackray fails to notice the movement on the surveillance cameras. He fails to notice that outside the wired fence of his office is a man in a padded leather jacket with a cap pulled down to conceal his face walking toward him.

At this moment, Thackray's absence from the sets of TV series *Healers* has triggered a mini chaos. But Thackray doesn't give a shit. The opposite could also be true. If a person says he doesn't give a shit, sometimes it could also mean that he cares deeply. A year ago when Thackray signed up for Medici pharmaceutical's TV drama the producers offered him a carte blanche; unrestricted freedom and authority in directing the series. Bullshit. Even Medici's low level executives have higher clearance than him and he is supposed to be running the show. The company's intrusions in the name of creative commerce, made worse by the cocky lead star's machismo, have transformed the series—which had started as a pungent portrayal of characters seeking redemption—into an unrecognizable pile of shit which he is increasingly embarrassed to own. Countless hours lost in living-eating-breathing fuck-loads of production, and a year later he realizes—in the words of a famous someone—it is the biggest cock-up ever! One thing is for sure, no one is going to be in a hurry to call *Healers* a masterpiece. Not in ten years. Not in fifty.

Thackray swallows a dose of paracetamol. The memory part is a fuzzy colloid as if he's looking in with a tracing paper against his eyes. He wants to wash his hands off the mess. But the company has made it clear: A 'legend' he may be, but he remains Medici property—legally—till he delivers their act.

It's clear that the world doesn't give a fuck about legends anymore.

Just write whatever comes to your head, dammit—Thackray forces his mind to think and fingers to write. To get a feeling of life in his head he unzips his pants and lets the heat off his crotch but instantly flops back with the exhaustion of a hundred years. *Dad—you are no legend*, as his daughter, Rathi, would say—*you can fool the world… not me, you are pathetic*. Rathi blames him for everything wrong in her life—drugs, shaky rehab, even for her bad choice in men. A 'self-centred schmuck' she calls him. He pretends the words do not twist his insides like a knife would. Maybe he should do the right thing by her and do something to make her happy, or at least less angry. She never forgave him for the humiliation of having to learn from a trending Twitter hashtag about his short-lived second marriage with a girl half his age. *Too messy, Danny boy*—his mother would say—*you are having rough days.*

A noise makes him stare into the black. There is something in the shadows. Watching? *Waiting!* This time the knock is louder.

'Just a minute,' he exclaims tucking his limp cock into his pants, 'What are you doing here?'

'I am sorry. Did I interrupt?'

'No. Nothing important. Have a seat. I thought it was my doctor. To tell the truth I am relieved it's not him!' Thackray finds his regular doctor, a closet doomsday prepper, too depressing since he diagnosed him as 'on verge of a meltdown accelerated by undiagnosable pains'.

'I will take only a moment…'

'Are you on Twitter?' Thackray watches the emaciated features across the table grin at the unexpected question. The smile almost tears the skin around the man's sharp cheekbone, like a death mask.

'Twitter? Not me!'

'The dead are trending. Landslide buries school bus—27 kids dead. Crashed MIG—11 dead. New Orleans shootout—49 dead—some singer is dedicating a song to the dead. What crap! The dead don't care.'

His eyes glued to his computer, Thackray does not see the other man withdraw a needle from his bag.

'Daughter hates Twitter, says people waste too much time on it eyy—'

The sting of the needle on his neck cuts him off mid-sentence. His muscles go gummy and he falls on the carpeted floor with a thump. He is unable to move and a phantom giant crab grips his body. Baffled, he watches the attacker retrieve a can from a bulky bag. Thackray instantly recognizes the stinky smell of petrol and his mind explodes in panic. The man douses the room with some fluid.

'Whatthfuck—' Words tumble out of the director's mouth in a rubbery mess, like bubbles in a slush bowl. The man ignores Thackray and retrieves a matchstick, lights it and throws the lit stick on the fuel soaked floor. It makes a sucking sound. A dull blue flame bursts up and moves toward Thackray. He chokes on rising bile and struggles to stand. But groggy legs unable to take his weight crumble and he falls backwards and crashes against the wall. The room is now full of smoke and the plastic casing of the computer is starting to melt. The man takes time to insert a bloated blue worm inside his left earhole.

'She is the queen. Full of eggs, very tough. Can survive extreme heat. Or fall… So what will it be, eh?'

With a loud noise the glass panes of the largest window shatters from the heat along the wall. Thackray feels his shoulders and back burn and the blaze on his face igniting his hair. Reality crashes in—tasting of blood and vomit and stone and he knows he is going to die. And then he can't take it anymore and jumps out. As he plummets twenty floors his last sane thought is that of a woman. Her eyes are blue with yellow specks, like his and his daughter's. Smiling, she beckons him down till razor branches slice his skin into fleshy slivers.

༶

Getting rid of the petrol can on the Link Road is not without risk. The man speeds his motorcycle and considers several options before he chooses the long abandoned beach stretch. A perfect setting for a city of sly air where every second man could be a murderer. By the time he is done, the sun is rising and with it the salt and his skin is sticky and swollen. He continues the rest of his journey unnoticed. Giant multi-utility vehicles filled with bikes. Several hoardings of a fizzy orange drink. An actor in expensive underwear on a billboard. A run-over dog, its guts spilled onto the road. More sky. Hippies with backpacks asking for a lift. Three miles down a stretch of the Dune's confusing geography, he steps into a habitation of bleak and unremitting ugliness. Choked with tinderbox constructions the streets open inwards into themselves, abysmal and continuous. He does not notice the spit, gum and used condoms which cover every inch of the pavement or the stagnant water solidifying in open drains or the mangy dogs biting each other for garbage morsels. He parks his motorcycle on the dirt-filled street and knocks on Hiri's door.

2

Ranganathan
Monday, 25 October
Somewhere along City Link Road, Exit 7

Ranganathan looks up to see the stars that have gone away and a yellow cresent moon looms out of focus. The boy's shrieks have also stopped. He relaxes. It is as dark as he wants it to be. He scrabbles at his car hood making pretence of going through the wiring. He keeps his eyes moving to make sure no one is watching him. There is no one around, no sign of any movement. It will be some time before anyone finds the little boy on the side of the road. Until then it is his secret.

He had wanted the little boy the instant he saw him playing alone by the roadside. He liked that the boy was noiseless and desperate enough to get into his car at the promise of a hot meal. He had a way of dropping his curly eyelashes and lifting them up which was sexy as hell. And had looked him directly in the eye the whole time he had him. He'd scarcely got his cock down the boy's throat before he had shot his load. He already misses the little boy, and wonders if the boy's family would file a police complaint after they see the thick wad of notes he stuffed in the boy's T-shirt. They hardly ever did. Ranga does not want to do anything that will draw attention to his car or himself, and so he takes the eastern link road, the arterial link to central city, hoping to avoid the rush hour. By the time he reaches the Medici Studio, he has the sly look of a man who knows his accurate worth and is fiercely committed to keeping it hidden.

Ranganathan, Head of Legal affairs and Brand Development at Medici Pharmaceuticals settles down in a private lounge of the studio for an urgent meeting with their brand ambassador, the movie star—Neville Valentine. He does not expect the meeting to be a pleasant one.

3

Neville Valentine
Monday, 25 October
Medici Studio

Valentine knows he is not mad. He 'knows' mad. But he is helpless in front of the angry rattlesnake which threatens to leap out of him any minute. The press interview is going from bad to worse. The reporter is a bitch who, he is sure, is out to get him and that makes him all the more mad.

'But Mr Valentine, there are accusations that Medici's ancillary drugs are too expensive for the public… I mean c'mon, what are we looking at? More than a lakh for a 20 c.c. dose? Are you serious!' Molly Limaye makes no effort to hide her disbelief.

'No average Indian can afford that except rich movie stars like you.' Molly Limaye is the Chief Reporter, General Affairs, Daily News. Valentine's assistant Binky Mendez had warned him Molly was not a fan and that she was unimpressed by his open vowelled baritone, his laban slash, the cock of his head or the raise of his brow.

'Look here, what are you trying to insinuate?' Dr Diaz, the chief architect of Medici's new Heal line, interrupts. 'Madam, funds are needed for hard-working biomedical research scientists. Medici's Heal drugs are the result of an intensive labour of five years. The public is intelligent enough to appreciate that even if journalists like you are not.' Dr Diaz has spent more than half of his life in tublight-lit interiors of a lab and he hates his work being questioned.

'So, the cost is justified?'

'Are you saying we should give it for free?' Dr Diaz retorts. 'I represent the brand and I know this much that the correct drug and the correct doctor alone can mend the failed machine—Medici has spent millions to develop the technology not to mention the years of hard work by our scientists.'

An unimpressed Molly surveys him as a cadaver for cause of death. 'According to reports, there are already several medicines in the market with similar characteristics but one tenth the cost.'

'Miss Limaye, clearly, you are clueless about science! We have created a primary weapon in our "war" against sickness. The diseases are more stubborn today. They cannot be cured by old formulae and drugs—we need to innovate and respond to this attack of disease with an assault. Win the war at all cost…'

'Win? A war? Wow, is this a war, Mr Valentine?' Molly Limaye throws the question at Valentine and Binky darts him a nervous glance. The star looks close to flipping out again. Last night at the party, Valentine had almost throttled one of his girlfriends—actress Kimmy White—when she refused to wear the garrotte-style collar with the nipple clamp. Tied her like a bale of hay with a riding crop, he had boasted about to Binky.

'I know you are trying to get me to say something so you can make a controversy about it. Do all journalists work like that now? Besides our motivations are not open to your opinion or interpretation. Let's not denounce a company which is doing good work.' Valentine's tone could cut paper.

'Heal's job is to repair the "defective" body parts,' Dr Diaz's voice is shrill as he butts in again, 'Medici has given Nature a "helpful" shove. No witches and faith-healers and herb-sellers here!'

'But isn't it a fact that Medici is facing allegations that this expensive medicine is not even new! That it's just a mild alteration of the actually existing form which as been in the market for last ten years? It is trending as #PharmaFraud and #UnfitForHumans!'

Both Valentine and Dr Diaz know too well what Molly was referring to. A set of tweets put out by an unverified handle @ICSW (International Clean Soil and Water NGO) were blaming Valentine of blindly lobbying for Medici. The tweets also accused Medici of refusing to share crucial trial details on its new Heal drugs. The @RCIM (Regional Court of Industrial Malpractice) somehow had got involved and then the @ICSW jumped in. Though Binky had set the bile spewing trolls on the @ICSW but some nationalist mob had joined in and then extreme right-wing folks and things had escalated way too quickly.

'The NGO's accusation is that Medici is not sharing trial details.'

'We think the NGO is misguided—and you are lazy. Every trial detail has been published if you had bothered to do your research! Medici puts healing above all—and our new version is stable hydroscopic form. It costs money to constantly update the research,' Diaz said hotly.

'Do you have any comments to make, Mr Valentine?'

'I am sorry the last question has been asked…'

'Mr Valentine, there is talk on the effectiveness of the vaccine being a lie and that the evidence is exaggerated by 115 per cent…'

Valentine doesn't realize that he is grinding his teeth. He wants nothing more than to smash Molly's smug face and crumple her into a ball.

'Mr Valentine, you are not answering my question—don't you think you owe people an explanation? Mr Valentine, are you okay? Sir?'

The anger is vast when it comes and it comes from everywhere. Every sound around Valentine has become particulate and the compression waves from the reporter's voice hit his temples like several tiny hammers.

'Pissssss off! Get lost!' The force of his movement sends his chair flying against the wall.

'You are telling me to get lost? It is my show, you know!'

'Go fuck yourself, bitch!'

'Please escort this reporter outside the Medici Studio. We have had enough of you for the day.' The menace in Binky's voice is clear.

The Medici Studio is cleverly camouflaged from the outside. Designed by a de-constructivist architect, it stands twelve stories high and straddles the Central City walkway—a megalith in concrete and glass. A fifteen-foot high three-thousand-pound installation—*HEALING FOR ALL*—is plonked in the centre of the lobby, lest one forgets the studio's purpose—creation of public campaigns (and now a TV series, movies later) to spread the 'Medici Philosophy of Healing'. Valentine thinks the years Medici has spent charging exhorbitant fees for its products should have given the company enough financial leeway to stick his face on a building that does not make him want to puke everytime he looks at it. Making bad even worse, is the sight of Ranganathan waiting for him like a badass wrestler past his badass days.

The two men eye each other warily. That their bond is not friendly is palpable. It is as between a man and his lender who has come to collect.

'Lets keep this civilized, Mr Valentine,' Ranganathan comes straight to the point, 'Your girlfriend Kimmy White's black eye and swollen face is all over the Internet. Our competitors are not blind. They will break the news to your adoring fans who probably think that you have come a long way from your coke whore-beating feather-headed cocksman days. How do you think this makes the brand look?'

'Fuck off. Don't forget I am the fucking jingle the public listens to when they buy your crappy pills...' Valentine retorts.

'It comes at a price, Mr Valentine. Yours is never to let your coke-whores and cocksman reputation be taken more seriously than the brand you represent. Our advertisers, our company partners—they feel uncomfortable. Medici feels if people start talking about the brand ambassador's lifestyle—it dilutes our brand right in the middle of our big launch! I would request you to go through the "moral clause" for such situations...'

'What the fuck is a moral clause.'

'Mr Valentine, I don't think you read the fine print of the "Medici Rule of Order". When you sent your "Acknowledgement" to become the prime agent of our "Prestige Product" that is Heal drugs, you also agreed that violation of rules according to the meaning assigned in clause 10.11(b) of the Terms and Conditions would amount to breach of the Moral clause and lead to termination of the contract.'

'You better be careful, Ranga,' Valentine's voice is plump with threat.

'I am sorry. I only say what the company wants. If you continue with this conduct then your status will change from "Brand Ambassador" to a "Liability"—and if that happens the company deals in a different way with liabilities elaborated in clause 10.32(a).'

'Are you threatening me?'

'Medici has a right to protect its commerce. Besides, aligning with Medici is not exactly a pact with the devil for *you* too have benefitted a great deal from our generosity. You never complained then!'

'I am not a circus monkey who will dance to the tunes of storekeepers like you—'

'Not just you—we all hop, skip, and jump like circus monkeys. The public is like annoying children. They can knock grand schemes to bits with their ham-handed fists if they feel fooled. It will hurt commerce if the public loses faith in you. Mr Valentine, we aren't here to make enemies with the press—them writing "Superstar flips out"—doesn't help us,' Ranga points an accusing finger at a website article.

'You think these pathetic haters who choose to assault me in articles make even a dent? They simply don't have enough fruit there to squeeze.'

'Valentine, you need to pay attention. You need to mind your place. Obey. You know the game. You are a Medici acquisition, to be owned or abandoned. Your current value determines your future possibilities. Medici's brand ambassador walking into the sunset with some rehab Jane is not part of the deal. You cannot let it go for a snatch even if she is fur-lined.'

'I am not as pussy blind as you think. Can you even find your dick under your blubber? Oh but you let someone else do that for you? Still making them work the nights to find your peanuts, eh?'

Valentine's words draw a very important line. The important message being imparted is that you better get the best of me or it will cost you. Ranga sucks in a breath and lets out a deep drawn sigh and walks off with a tight smile.

The misgivings had begun when, months ago, Ranganathan was hand-picked by Medici management to scrutinize the TV project *Healers*. To be fair, it was Medici's desperate step to restore a measure of goodwill with the public in the face of relentless bad press surrounding their troublesome movie star brand ambassador. The brief to Ranga was clear. Medici wanted to be rid of the increasingly out of control brand ambassador, Valentine. Shareholders had hinted they were unwilling to put in anymore capital and the management was worried—'We need to create a positive image'. They had told him, 'You are a lawyer…find a way out!' Years ago when he had joined Medici, his main job had primarily been to monitor the digitization of Land Records for Medici. That he could easily dispose of decency, and legalities, in favour of the company's interests was useful in acquiring landed property for Medici. But this was a different matter altogether. Valentine's contract was water tight and getting out of it was easier said than done. Unless…his plan worked.

A knot begins to work behind his temples, as Ranga drives out of the studio. The world outside has drained to grey impressions and the winds are howling between the seams in the sky. But that does not stop drifters from spilling into the streets. The lucky ones had squeezed into cosy cement crotches formed where flyovers met giant cement pillars holding their weight up, and children had crammed under the temporary plastic tarps erected outside side shops lining the roads. Ranga is unable to shake off the feeling of being pinned in the cross-hairs of hidden danger. A slim boy peers from under a transparent polythene sheet at his car his tiny hand curled into cups. He has knowing eyes and a probing nose. Ranga feels a familiar lurch when his soft fingers graze his palm for the loose change.

'I do you now? In car, mister? I'll be fast, mister—guarantee satisfy!' sneers the boy jerking his cupped palm crudely. The coarse words hang in the air but before Ranga could realize, the mite disappears into a crack under the flyover with the money.

'Thiefing punk!' He curses, and almost immediately notices another boy standing all alone under the flyover. The little boy's unexpected beauty makes him gasp in delight.

4

Kimmy White
Monday, 25 October
Le Bon Goût, Grand Rue

All the happening girls ate at Le Bon Goût on the Grand Rue of the southern suburbs. That is the chief reason why Kimmy White prefers the overpriced restaurant despite the fact that she cannot afford a single square meal there. But as usual, she will settle for a coffee with the free cookies. She has patiently waited till after 10 p.m. for the happy meals' hour when choice items are discounted. Her studio canteen offers affordable meals but for a young, upcoming actress eating is a much lower priority than keeping up the appearance. Kimmy likes being recognized by the 'it' crowd which frequents this place—it's like entering an exclusive club of people in Hugo Boss and Jimmy Choo with verified Twitter accounts, strong opinions, and who party at Drai and Drai, Reina and such. Le Bon Goût had established itself as a classy restro-bar and Kimmy White in her figure-hugging Jovani ripoff completely fitted in. Although her gorgeous serpentine locks were uncombed and her eyes were almost haggard, her beauty could make one gasp. Today the heavy make-up around the eyes hidden behind the large Cavalli sunglasses is not for purely aesthetic reasons. Last night's bondage confinement game at the party had gone way out of hand. Neville Valentine had gotten carried away as the 'dominant' and almost took her face off with the whip.

'Table for one?' The hostess is soft and inviting as she is chaperoned to a cosy corner.

'How are you today? What would you like?' a kind lilt, a practiced croon to secure a successful transaction and Kimmy almost feels a lump in her throat. It is exactly the kind of place she would have liked to own if she had the money: classy décor, soft music, and lots of expensive wine. The caramel cookie is crunchy with pistachio as she takes a big bite.

'Miss Kimmy?' An officious looking man summons her with a peremptory gesture.

'Yes? Is there a problem?' she notices his uniform.

'Miss, we have a complaint from the Eau de Parfums section that two very, very expensive Burberry perfume bottles are missing and a Valentino pushup bra is missing from the Exotique section. We wanted to know if by, ahem, any chance, you happen to have any items in your possession?'

It was not a question.

'Why would you say that?'

'Would you want to check your bag, Miss White…,' his head inclined at a determined angle, '…with the festive rush there is always possibility of confusion—people forget…'

'Nonsense! Do you know who I am? I am a regular customer here. To think that I made a mistake…! I know what I buy—oh…oh my god I just forgot about—Oh My God—this is so embarrassing—this has never happened before… I have had such a busy day at the sets. I was probably thinking of my lines and then…hey, wait a minute… I hope you don't think I took it on purpose! You know it is a mistake, don't you?'

There is a long silence from the security officer's side. The silence could have meant anything. 'Miss White, we would like you to come with us. And return the items you have taken from the Exotique section by mistake.'

The security officer's grey moustache bobbed commandingly on his upper lip as he spoke.

'Sure! How long will this take?'

'Just as long as you take.' He shot back tersely. Kimmy responded by girdling her face into an unreadable code. At nineteen, she looked about as strong-willed as a creeping holly. Her vacant expression made her look like the sort of girl who can never prioritize matters. So, she comes across as either too stubborn or too silly to people. But people often rue this premature judgement. For Kimmy has a honed mind, which she prefers to hide under a misty-eyed vagueness. This way no one expects much from her and it takes off the pressure to deliver. And no one sees her coming when she does. With as much nonchalance as she can muster, Kimmy picks her large red bag and walks behind the officer. When she notices youngsters from the adjoining table pointing their mobile cameras at her, she dashes out of Le Bon Goût.

When Kimmy White had rented the apartment at Glen Heights several months ago she had never imagined she would be thrown out in this manner, based on a viral video.

'We have packed all your belongings. You can check your rooms before you move out.' The landlord's daughter informs her in a curt tone.

'Move out?'

'We all know the reason. Let's not make this any difficult.'

'But where will I go? I am entitled to a notice…'

'Your act at the mall is all over the Internet. It's gone viral.' The sister spits out the word 'viral'.

'It was a mistake from their end—the manager apologized to me!'

'We aren't saying anything,' the brother's voice is small, 'but you are an actress and this sort of stuff sticks. It was very tough for me to convince this society to let us rent out to an actress. And now this has happened. It's best if you moved out.'

Kimmy wants to protest. The young boy was once a fan with a crush on her and had fought against the apartment complex's rules to let her move in. But words get stuck in her throat as they face each other in an embarassed silence.

'Where will you go?' the boy's gaze is fixed at a point above her shoulder.

'I was in any case going to move out to my new flat,' she said with a toss of her head, and adds, 'I will send someone to pick my stuff.' It is not until she is safely ensconsed in the interiors of the car, her face hidden with a giant scarf, that she lets hot tears roll down her cheeks.

Shitty armpit people.
Shitty, shitty, shitty, town.

The taxi drops her to the western part of the city a good two hours later. Right in the middle of a colourless parade of 'everything under one roof' dollar stores with plastic frontage. Her mother's old flat, on the first floor of West colony, was part of a one time alimony pay-off from her first husband. Litter piles on the sides of the road—filled with empty pizza boxes, used condoms, torn newspapers, and a good population of feral life forms. Yet the street has a vital commitment to surviving at any cost.

When she wakes up she realizes it had not been a bad dream. But Kimmy doesn't waste much time thinking of her loss. She dials her agent Mey's number to tell her that she is ready to take up the TV role. A day ago, Kimmy had told Mey to take a hike for the same.

'Good decision, girl! So, what if it's not a speaking part but it is a Medici project! And besides you can do only so much with a career based on a pair of titties—girl, you will fry them with your salt!'

The compliment was given in all sincerity by Mey who is sure that 'lukin salty' is the brilliance every actress strives for. That Kimmy thinks of Mey as a greasy sort with limited intelligence and questionable integrity is something she keeps to herself in order to keep the relation functional till the woman is of use to her. It's a small role but Kimmy tells herself it doesn't matter. She does not have any abiding ambition to make it as an actress anyway.

Kimmy's life represents every purposeful girl's dream, a counter's breadth between obscurity and stardom. Till the fateful day when Dinesh Thackray's glazed eye fell on her stunning body. The special moment which propelled her from an anonymous existence into a fairytale world came rather fast, in the form of quick nuptials with the aging and completely smitten legend. But fate intervened in the form of a unexpected sexual rendezvous with the handsome and extremely wealthy superstar, Neville Valentine. Kimmy's understanding of her social coordinates underwent a drastic shift. The affair got Kimmy her first taste of the good life, the glitzy parties, the expensive gifts and the crazy, if not increasingly violent, fetish sex. She called in the lawyers, with generous help from Valentine, to help her wriggle off the nuptial hook with the old Thackray. Kimmy had finally emerged from a fug of confused existence to exciting new possibilities, mansions on the city hills with her own quay. But life has scant regard for plans. Kimmy has sensed an alarming chill in Valentine's ardour for her.

The grey shadows around her changed places with the sinking sun. It was time. The room was filled with labrys axes, caducei wands, ankhs and a giant sistrum full of pleasure and pain implements—riding crops, floggers and switches, bottles of lube, blindfolds, and various other accessories. Little boxes were meticulously labelled with hand-written notes like 'Nipple Clamps', 'Vibrators', 'Restraints' and 'Gags'. Kimmy fished out from under a silk scarf a colophoned book. The book's cover was trident-shaped and pockmarked with hundreds of tiny hexagons. It was the grand book of neo-thaumeturgy. She leafed to the chapter on 'augury and prophecy'. For those unfamiliar with the trends of neo-thaumeturgy, it proposes some unconventional interpretations of the spiritual-material world on the basic aphorism: build your hatred...and take revenge on those...who trespassed against you. No one knows when they came into perceptible existence but the neo-thaumeturgist sect has been around for long on the fringes of urban society.

It's a small elite fellowship of men and women, a tenacious off-shoot of Fet Life, a secretive social media club, of people who have a passion for pain in a way normal people did not understand. Followers believe the path to wish fulfillment is the moment of climactic instant when the mind is totally blank and one can penetrate into the mystic world and be one with the supreme power when in a state of extreme pain. The seconds which follow are believed to be entirely devoid of thought, the state of brief mental vacuum are the most powerful moments to make the 'wish'. Kimmy took off her skirt and gagged her mouth. The copper container retrieved from its dark confines held a black shaft. With its small, slim leather end she hit her thighs with quick thirty strokes, at equal intervals. When it is over she doubles over with pain. Wiping the vomit sticking to her face, she smiles. The ritual will ensure her the wealth of a powerful man according to the book. She is still smiling when the phone rings. Kimmy White recognizes the high pitched voice on the other side.

'Miss White, congratulations for becoming part of Medici family. I was sure you will come around. Have you had the time to go over my proposition—my condition to amplify your role in *Healers*—to make it prominent...you will have to do the following—'

During the length of Ranganathan's three-minute call, different aspects of her expressions gain and lose prominence. The result is a face steeped in a compound of vulnerability and calculation. Kimmy's eyes sparkled in the dark room. The question is not whether Valentine would give her the life she wants. The question is what all she will have to do to ensure it happens.

5

Neville Valentine
Monday, 25 October
Basement cellar, 555 Neverland

Valentine finds foreplay a waste of time. With an impatient movement, he straddles Rathi. She shivers and sinks down on her knees. He crouches like a bulldog on his legs and brings his body tight against her. Putting his powerful legs around her hips, he pulls back, raises his hips and penetrates her, first slightly, then deeper, pushing his last inches in her till his penis runs out of room. Rathi is full of him and he works his hips unsparingly without giving her any time between one stroke and the next. The murky sky transforms their nakedness into a thing of decadent beauty, Schiele's lovers. The nature of space around them is two-dimensional as if the air has become flat to emphasize that there is no universe outside their senses. They finish and start again. Valentine can't help but stare at her as she spreads her legs and pushes her hips slightly forward, the gold specks in her grey eyes glinting.

'Don't…' her voice picks up an edge when he touches her, 'I will give you a hundred miles an hour but don't reach for me at this speed it will hurt us both!' She laughs a deep throaty laugh, a golden laugh that is rich and full like she is. Rathi is tall, almost 5'11", with long legs and big beautiful feet. Her skin is brown velvet, smooth and soft, yet taut, it glows with the shine of life. Her neck tapers to good strong shoulders almost masculine in their form and her big breasts sit high on her chest, full and firm. When she is done he moves like a man who is performing his favourite role. With his penis in a semi-erect state he dabs a thick lubricant on his index finger. Positioning the two digits in a decent grip on the base of his cock, he slowly slides his hand up to the head of the penis. Releasing the grip of his hand, he slides to the base and repeats the movement to increase the blood flow.

The contours of their bodies blend and move like two fish halves swirling away and into each other converging and seeping into one another—a blurry pattern of her swirls and his rectangles. However much he sleeps with her there is a whole part of Rathi which remains untouched. For Valentine, that is a huge turn-on. He leans to the right and touches a discreetly placed lever on the side of the bed. A wall panel swivels open revealing a hidden chamber, concealed behind an empty space. It leads to a hidden subspace and is designed in a way that makes it impossible to find unless one knows it's there. A soundproof 1,800-square-foot subspace studio equipped with all the latest accoutrements of kinky sex, a jail cell for confinement play, a medical room for doctor–patient fantasies filled with a selection of toys and props, bondage tables, wall shackles and a spanking bench. Valentine calls the dungeon his labour of love. Rathi stares open-mouthed when he shows off an organized array of pleasure and pain implements—riding crops, floggers and switches, bottles of lube, blindfolds, and various other accessories.

Valentine had warned Rathi. He was not sure whether she could handle the level of pain. But she had decided to give it a try. As an initiation, he negotiates a scene that will involve impact play, which means he will hit her with a cane, a paddle or his hand on her thighs, buttocks, back and arms. The plan is for her to warm up, gradually escalating the impact of his strokes to prepare her skin for the hard blows. She agrees to five strokes of a solid wood cane, two-and-a-half centimetres in width. At first impact, he hits her softly on the upper thighs. She realizes he has abandoned the warm-up—her flesh starts to welt immediately. Things move too fast, and she looks insecure about not being able to play hard enough. Rathi asks him to turn down the intensity. The second time he hits her harder.

'No. Stop! I can't—'

But it's as if he can't hear her. He hits her three more times. And she thinks she is going to vomit.

'Stop, STOP—NOW!'

'C'mon, you don't want to disappoint me, do you?' His eyes are glazed and he plunges into her very hard. There is an alarming edge about his expression and at that moment self-preservation seems to kick into Rathi. She hits him on his back but he continues to thrust inside her without releasing her throat. With a bit of struggle Rathi pushes back and they both slip off the chair and into the pool with a splash, making the water fall over the railing. The cold water revives Valentine who instantly loosens his grip.

'This is sick! Who does this! I can't—what the fuck is wrong with you, Valentine?' Rathi screams sliding of the pool edge and ripping off the towel to cover herself.

'I am sorry—I am—did I hurt you? I—don't know what happened to me...'

'Leave me alone—I don't want to do this ever. You are going fucking insane, Valentine. You are going completely mad. Get help.' Rathi struggles to breathe. She opens her mouth to lash out but he has already moved back with the strained fluidity of a beast forced to abandon its prey.

Of course he is not going mad.

Valentine knows what it is like to 'go mad'. He had seen his mother go mad. Everyone called her a mad coke whore. At the age of fifteen, he had seen her corpse being dragged out of the sea—a failed career? An affair gone sour? No money to buy drugs? He does not recall. Nor care. What he knows is that he is not mad that way. His madness is designed to keep him sane.

In front of him on the giant flickering mainframe, a man with deadpan eyes frantically drilled into a woman in throes of a fake orgasm. Valentine doesn't feel a thing. He holds his cock in his hand. It feels corpulent. Maybe it is dying…he had heard dead tissue becomes heavier. He taps a reddish ash from his stoked cigarette into the weed colloid, a tricky manoeuver he has perfected to maximize the taste of nicotine to its very threshold. His eyes stream from the concentrated acetic bite. A moment later there is a new shrewdness to his character, a sharpness to his pose. But the feeling of his skull caving in doesn't entirely leave him.

6

Rathi Thackray
Monday, 25 October
Medici Studio

When did she get so abnormal? She had acted like a bitch in heat. Disgust and shame washes through Rathi. Her Prince Charming is a douchebag, a selfish sick prick. But also the greatest fuck of her life. She feels disgusted that a part of her wants to be his prey, to be torn apart and eaten by him. Holding her scarf closer to her face, she steps into the crowd briefly relishing the anonymity of mixing in a swelling populace returning home after a hard day's work. She walks past the precocious movie-kids clutching cotton candy cones and side-steps the glaze-eyed gum chewing line dancers going clap and stomp on toe-dance. The colourful dervishes of sweat do nothing to restore her. Rathi is furious with Valentine for making her feel cheap and powerless. But she cannot escape the fact that she herself allows him a strange dominance over her. It was like a relapse after rehab—and the drug was more of a mind fuck. That he is false yet she fastens to him in an unnatural bondage. It is almost as if she is back on coke. Her attraction for Valentine—what was that song: *'I don't need a cure/I will just stay addicted/and hope I can endure'*—something like that.

She should have dumped him with the drugs, which was the reason why they had got together to begin with. It was not like he had not warned her. But she had been turned on by his *'I may fuck you and strangle you at the same time'* line. Drugs and sex, the primeval concordance which existed between the brain and neurochemicals involved in both addictions, so she could actually blame it on the overload of dopamine, oxytocin and vasopressin in her head. There are two kinds of men, the boys who never grow up, never get serious and cream eternally on themselves and their machines. They are about numbers and variety. And men who appreciated women for more than their flexibility and mouth suction. Valentine, she had thought, was the third kind, the sort she had never met. Maybe she wanted some spice in her boring life. And what is wrong with that anyway? At thirty-five, she is old enough to know, isn't she? Stabbing the soft garden mud with the sharp heel of her sandal, Rathi gets ready for her audition.

Scene 32, Healers
Shooting in progress

'H-h-h-hey! Where d'ya think you are goin Elsa?' *Bela slurs through her flabby lips and jabs Rathi's chest with an extravagantly theatrical gesture.*

Words tumble from Rathi's mouth in a well-rehearsed rush of barely distinguishable syllables, 'As sure as my name is Elsa, I am my mother's daughter and I'm sick of your shit, old witch... your game is up.'

'Get her, Rocky... get that girl,' *Bela barks an order. Fingering a chunky gold chain around his neck declaring Rocky is King, a pitbull shaped actor approaches Rathi with exaggerated menace.*

'I don't pay you to stuff your face with booze and flesh... teach her a lesson—Rocky get Elsa off me!' *Rathi swiftly presses a sharp knife on Bela's throat.*

'Try stopping me, you old witch!'

'And—cut! Break for lunch. Back on the sets in one hour. But before that—hey, pay attention people—' Chief Associate Director Aslam Kapadia yells at the TV crew with a face which carries the burden of an unappealing persona. He wears his designation as a badge to bully those at a disadvantage specially when Dinesh Thackray is not around. A large nose stopped short midway of its growth till it perhaps continued to grow into itself. The chin protrudes horizontally from the jaw giving his tapering face a formidable dimension.

'Everyone, remember, before you depart to feed your guts—all your phones should be placed—HERE—with me. If I catch any of you with as much as a wire this is the last you will see of the Medici Studio—or any studio—you will be blacklisted forever, so don't say Mr Kapadia didn't warn you—NO PHONES ON MY SETS. PERIOD.'

'Cut them some slack—they are doing double shifts!' says Rathi.

'Miss Thackray...' Aslam frowns and she knows it's a struggle for him to keep his misogynist streak under control. He exchanges a what-the-fuck-is-this-bitch-talking-about look with Stud. With dragon tattoos on his oxen-neck, Stud looks like the sort who can't tell the difference between polite behaviour and a sexual come-on and may mistake a handshake for an invitation to bed. In a weird way, Aslam and Stud could be soulmates, she thinks and grins.

'Miss Thackray, if I let them carry their phones, they will leak pictures of the set, the costumes, the lines—you cannot trust anyone these days.' Aslam's combative eyes reduce to pointy blacks. Clearly his problem should be everyone's problem. Rathi is sorry she opened her mouth.

'They call me a fascist pig behind my back. Allah knows I will never ever keep a cent to myself which does not belong to me. It is haram with us you know.'

Rathi meets such men every day. The misogynist victim types who think the world is unfair and slow in reacting to their greatness. And feel attacked by any attempt to show them their error or in the face of genuine talent. She knows Aslam is not above waving his religion card to be compensated for his constant frustration.

'I am stuck with shitty production control. I got a gold medal in my college project for direction—but who gives a damn?' Aslam tries to keep the envy for her father from creeping into his voice. Rathi sighs. Her father has the ability to do that. Fuck everyone's happiness without raising a finger. She will be damned if she will take the blame for his shit.

'I made a legitimate storyboard, like they taught us in college but Mr Thackray threw my storyboard-sketches into the dustbin! I sense so much opposition to my creative process—people like us…'

'Shut the fuck up, Aslam! Use your damn head and get a perspective. If he calls your creative process shit then maybe it really is.'

Aslam looks like he has been stabbed in the eye.

'Oh and I think you suffer from a bipolar victim perspective which I am sure will soon be replaced by a bout of manic narcissism. So, you will be fine. Hell, I should be the one with bloody victim issues because my dad is making me audition for a role in his film! So you can stop your fucking rant,' she says and walks off. Rathi is more rude than she intended to be, but this is all the manic narcissism she can take in a day. The rumble of the studio-generator stutters and she finds herself in a corridor with cables running everywhere like a subcutaneous network of wires, feeding, gorging off each other. It's bad enough that she cannot breathe, speak, swallow or hear anything outside of her own painfully thudding heartbeat.

That's when she gets a call informing her that their had been a fire at her father's office. There were no bodies found. The police wants to know if she knew his whereabouts. He had apparently not been seen since the fire.

'Do let us know if your father contacts you.'

7

Thoolsa and Jhoompa
Monday, 2 November
Block 2, Jagdamba Forest Area

Thoolsa and Jhoompa sprint through the abandoned little forest stretch as fast as their legs can carry them. The place abounds in cooked and sometimes uncooked dead remains of chicken, goat, fish and fowl dumped carelessly into the jungle by the lazy kitchen boys of the several film units who shoot nearby. The breathless boys know this was the best place to find what they were looking for. Sometimes, they also managed to lay their hands on a straying egret which they killed with sharp stones or a solitary chicken but what they were really looking for was lots of live bait for their weekend fishing expedition.

The succulent fishes of the Dambi have acquired a special taste for the prize they were after, big fat juicy maggots, the luscious bloated larvae of blue flies that lay their eggs on the carcass of dead animals. The boys intend to use the bait to lure the highly prized Bombay ducks which abound in the cold black waters of the lake. Seven-year-old Thoolsa and his ten-year-old brother, Jhoompa, run into the thickly wooded Jagdamba forests hoping for a bumper catch, it being monsoon the season when blue flies lay their eggs. And by the way things looked, it could be their lucky day. As they ran down the familiar patch of the dry woods they could hardly contain their excitement. Lying a few feet off a forest path inside the broken down wall of the open film studio compound there was a pulsating seething fur of white. Jhoompa saw it first and yelled at Thoolsa who whistled sharply, his mouth opening into a perfect 'o'. The fattest juiciest white maggots on a mound of rough sods of turf loosely covered with beech cuttings. Panting with emotion their polythene bags waving in the air, the happy boys dashed to the spot, at once pulling and prodding the turf. They were not put off by the terrible stench which seemed to be emanating from the maggot-filled spot, but instead impatiently pushed off the chunky roots and driftwood to claim their precious prize. Until Thoolsa caught sight of the decomposing fingers attached to the remains of a hand on the other end. Their fishing expedition ripped short, the brothers left everything including their fishing lines and polythene bags and carefully packed tiffins and ran out of the woods with ghostly expressions.

8

Dorab Silva
Monday, 2 November
Block 2, Jagdamba Forest Area

Ring ring ringgg—
Ring ring ringgg… Ring ring ringgg…ringgg—
Has it been twenty rings? Or more? He has lost count.
Ring ring ringgg…
Someone is really dedicated.

But Police Officer Dorab Silva refuses to budge. He should not even be at home. The original plan was to pick up a refill for his sinus medicine prescription and then to buy the best piece of fresh trout in the market, and that way he aimed to kill two birds with one stone or whatever. After that he planned to spend the day in his living room, watching his favourite movies and drinking chilled beer. It was one of those days when he felt so content he would not even mind the really big crackers going off near his window. But the day was not going according to plan. Silva looks at his fish tank and observes that the captive koi is about the only thing alive in the world that he cared for. The fresh water around the fish is clouded with fresh shit. The koi stares back, shitting with greater might—its arrogant eyes content with the knowledge that he will clean its shit.

'Pretentious little fuck,' Silva swears. The koi jumps in the tank when the phone rings again.

Ring ringgg... Ring ringgg...ringgg—

RRRRiiiinggg—

Ignoring the phone, Silva shifts his gaze at the pigeon-shit caking the sill. He is thinking of placing a fake cat to keep them from shitting on the wood-work. He shuffles to the ice-box looking for beer but stops to re-arrange the magnets on the fridge, moving them around. Word forms break apart and he knew he was trancing out into the half-hypnotized state which he had cultivated with the help of his shrink to deal with his trauma. The brief time he had consulted the therapist after his wife's death he had been advised to let the intuitive part of his mind unlock itself to release the pain and to let his mind rise to a height of ten feet. He had been told the painless zone hovers there. A certain 'painless zone' where memories do not lead to pain. Thoughts come and go uninvited. And some other unwanted stuff too. He has since dumped the shrink, but trouble was that the trance button seemed to switch on and off on its own. And there are days when the intuitive part of him goes so high up he is sure he will not be able to find it even with a search party.

Ring ring ringgg—

Ring ringg—rrrriiiinnn

Mr Dedicated is not giving up. Silva reckons it must be trouble ringing. In his experience, people don't try as hard when the news is good.

※

A highly decomposed corpse was discovered by village boys out on a fishing expedition and Silva was to accompany the physician to supervise the collection of the bodily remains. He leaves his house at 3 p.m. and in a little over an hour he had joined the team at the

Jagdamba forest stretch behind the film studios. Not quite thirty-eight years old yet, Silva had a lean and tightly muscular body and an assurance which came with experience. He thought of himself as a good judge of character and refused to be ever daunted by another man. A shit luck case is completely another matter.

Near the old scarred pines, he turns off the engine not because he wants to walk the half a mile to ground zero but because his eight-year-old car has begun to steam. He walks to the rear of his car, lays down on his stomach and begins pulling out all the grass which was touching the car's hot exhaust system from below. The lightest brush of his arm against the car's door leaves him smelling of varnish. The much-needed car service that was due months ago can no longer be delayed. Silva looks up at the cloudy sky and feels the bloody coppery taste in the back of his mouth that always amplified as the clouds advanced. If he does not hurry, rains would finish all business with the dead body without him even starting.

The body of the late middle-aged man is lying on his back, fully clothed and with his head wrapped in towelling. The blanket covering the body has gained a film of beaded glass from the misty weather. The body had been long disintegrating. A forensic officer is diligently removing the turf cuttings and sprays of thick smelly breech wood stuck in the stiff fingers, stopping to allow photographs to be taken from every angle. The medical examiner has declared it too late to measure the loss of body temperature and that rigor mortis must have come and passed off again long before. Given the condition of the body, the officers have promptly set about photographing and the young medical examiner is making scientific notes of the dead body.

'Double-tapped in the neck and spine and then thrown down. Some bloody joker was very determined,' observes the medical examiner.

'Look at the maggot-fest!' Silva holds a swirling bloated maggot in his hand.

'At least nine or ten days, but probably not more than that. Lucky buggers had a feast... I don't mean that of course, all this is bloody sad,' the examiner quips while nudging the body with the tip of his boot.

'Here come the vultures,' Junior Police Officer Gouda, a brutish, thickset man with a scarred cheek and a gruff approach, said pointing at the TV crews' trucks trying to manoeuvre their way into the secluded stretch.

'Disgusting. Bloody flesh-eaters,' the medical examiner said, 'these maggots—are the bluebottle calliphora erythrocephalus...'

'I have seen how quickly maggots will eat up flesh. A body can be reduced to this state in as less as six days,' Silva cuts in.

'True. I have preserved samples because the maggots of other flies of this family have different hatching timings but are not dissimilar to the naked eye.' The medical examiner reminds Silva of the younger himself, when he was a restless boy with frayed cuffs and an impatience that belied his habitual dreamy half-focused appearance. Nineteen years in the force has morphed his temperament into a permanent state of edginess and cynicism.

'So, when do you think this happened?' Silva asks with barely concealed impatience.

'Well, the ordinary life history of a bluebottle is quite simple. The eggs are laid in daylight—usually sunlight and in warm weather, and they hatch on the first day itself. The first instar maggot sheds its skin in 8–14 hours. And the second instar after 2–3 days. The third instar, which is the fisherman's maggot, feeds voraciously for 5–6 days before going into the pupa stage. Still quite helpless really—just a baby—' The medical examiner explains the maggots in great detail, like people who talk about everything so as to not be accused of missing a point. Silva holds up a stick with some more bloated maggots squirming on the other end.

'These are mature, elderly, fat and lazy third stage maggots. I think the eggs were laid 9–10 days earlier. And if you give the bluebottles a little more time to get inside the body of this man then I'd say…' The examiner talks into the memo-scriber so as to not pollute the truth with the narnias of imagination. Silva notices the breech leaves sticking out from under the dead body and looked around. There were no breech trees in the vicinity.

'I think because of extensive decomposition and maggot infestation we should do some preliminary examination of the exposed parts of the body as they are right now.' Silva lightly touches the pool of thick chocolate blood under the corpse's medulla oblongata. The small bones on the larynx were crushed on one side.

'Well…' At this point an electric bolt lit up the sky scouring the area with purple and pink. In its glare, the labouring trees look like they were pointing fingers and from the north end of the forest came a grinding crackling crash.

'It's going to rain, boss,' Gouda says and then corrects himself, 'Flood.'

'Better hurry then or the maggots, along with their dinner, will only be good enough for stew. The dirt's rising,' Silva looks at the sky and back at the corpse.

'Okay. So, we have a smashed pumpkin head with his arms and legs bent in a way they aren't supposed to. How did he get here? Dumped or fell? It could have been that the body had fallen from a height from the film studio.' Gouda has a lot of suggestions.

'Except that it could have also happened from a direct hit. It's possible that someone hit him on the neck from behind… could be a punch—of course all this is premature—but no one falls this way without being pushed,' the medical examiner sounds ambiguous.

'Felled with a blow and then pushed?'

'It's possible that he sustained this injury while falling down, but I will have to look closer. This will take a few days and even then we will only have probabilities. The state of the body is really bad, as you can see officer.'

'Will he fall apart if you turn his head?' Silva wants to know.

'Would you like to or should I do it for you?' The examiner turns the body and both the policemen inspect the caved-in head.

'But look at this...a weird constellation of keratoid scars on his back and butt. These here appear old, but they look like they have been treated. And then there are fresh ones. But seems superficial, no real damage to the epidermal tissue—' the examiner declares.

'Maybe Mr Maggot did it to himself—don't be shocked, you won't believe some of the things I have seen people get high on in this city. There will be a day when people will suck their own brain just to feel something—anything! This man... I think I've seen him, Gouda...no, I can't be sure since they all look alike in magazines—' said Silva.

'On a magazine? Boss, you have seen Mr Maggot here on some magazine?' Gouda shoots a glance at his boss.

'Okay, this may be of interest to you. Prescription drugs Adderall and Klonopin for panic attacks and fear seizures were both found in his wallet.' The medical examiner adds another bit of information.

'Wait... I think I have seen his pictures in magazines—with film stars and stuff—the one with the really pretty daughter, an actress—the one who is dating that—' Silva squints his forehead trying to force out the memory.

'Mr Maggot has a name?'

'The maggots have not got to his face—oh bugger—wait! It's the director with the name like a fish...' Silva snaps his finger, 'It's that film director—Thackray—Dinesh Thackray... Yes that's him!'

'Are you sure it is him? How do you know? You don't even watch films,' Gouda smirks.

'But I read the fucking papers! He has been all over the papers for making some big television film. And if what they say about his ego is true then there is no way he would have taken that dive of his own free will. Someone must have lent Mr Thackray, if its indeed him, a helping hand.'

'I don't think he has been reported missing, boss.'

'I am not surprised. I read he likes to take off alone—some creative process shit. He is considered a kind of legend. They reported a fire at his office a week ago. I heard that it was completely burnt down. There was no one there in the office at the time. Come to think of it, you can see his office building from here... some fifty paces ahead.' Silva measures the distance with his eyes.

'Do you think he jumped to escape the fire?'

'Mighty long jump for a corpse if he was dead already, boss.'

'Bloody motherfucker, Gouda! This place is full of animals, dogs and foxes at night. Some animal may have dragged him—'

'Sad. All that money... glory... and he ends up as maggot lunch. No fucking justice in life.'

'Justice? You get justice in the afterlife. All you have in this world is the fucking law and some bloody joker always forgets that. By then some poor sod has paid for it.' Silva says while looking at the remains of Dinesh Thackray.

9

Binky Mendez
Monday, 2 November
Medici Studio

Years ago Binky had earned Valentine's lifetime of goodwill with an act of devotion: a virulent critic tweeting a damning article on the star found himself the object of net vendetta of such prurient nature that he had to close his account and tender a personal apology to the star. That Binky is a homosexual is an open secret. His crisply ironed tiger stripes don't distract one from his parachute-like ears, a chin perpetually tucked into the folds of his neck and a face that was a harvest moon, not just its fullness and roundness but how it was mottled, cratered and dappled with acne scars. An obsessive streak marks his character, and a near pathological loyalty to Valentine. Anyone foolish enough to cross him would get subjected to a tidal wave of bile that could gag the thickest skinned. And that would be just the beginning. Binky Mendez takes his job seriously, and he knows that Valentine is walking the thin line. It's his duty to see to it that he does not get into too much trouble.

⚜

Medici Studio,
Valentine's vanity van
Script-reading session

'Mr Valentine... I just want to know if you have read the script—'
The stunt director mumbles all the while refusing to make eye contact with Valentine.

'Binky, tell him to shut up. Why the fuck do I need to read a script for a fight scene, Mr Stunt Director? I'm Valentine.'

'As you say, sir. But you should know that it's an imaginary fight scene. The sequences include brutal fights, it's rather fetishistic and personal. I've sent you the popular War Game XII video—it will give you an idea about the scene. Just watch it...it's got more than twenty techniques that could be shot in one take. It's really frenetic...'

'Fuck off! I want slow and dramatic.'

'But the onslaught has to be non-stop—that's how Medici wants—'

'No, you bastard! It's not what Medici wants. Its what I want. Put in clear breaks. Dirty sex. And why the fuck do I have to look like a cadaver—will some fuckball tell me?' Valentine was in a bad mood.

'The emotion of the film is blue. Your character is under constant threat of being murdered—Mr Thackray said it has to be stylized. The action workshop he mentioned would help you to—'

'What the fuck is an action workshop? Fuck off or I am going home!'

'I think that's enough! If Mr Valentine wants more colour then he gets more. All right? Please leave the van. And send Boy in.' Binky Mendez's militant voice was a clear signal for the stunt director to scamper out.

Boy, an adept derma-specialist, walks in armed with colouring emulsions, pigments wax, overlay stains and assorted cosmetics. He has high cheekbones and a nose which ends on either side in a pair of deep whorls underlined by thick lips and possesses a restless demeanour of those often consumed by causes or deep passions. Boy is a whiz with body make-up and his hands splotched brown with regular use of chemical have aged more than his face and the rest of his body. It was Binky who had discovered him during a brief stay at a skin treatment centre where he was taking training in skin healing techniques. Valentine takes off his silk robe and lies down on his stomach.

'Make me shine, Boy. Varnish me into a sultan.'

Boy masterfully creates tendons and ligaments on the Superstar's body and with the other hand removes the cracks and peels at the flexion points on the star's skin. With thin slivers of paint on the star's pale thighs, he sketches out a masterful likeness of rippling muscles. Deftly creaming the star's broad back he keeps aside areas blank for some fine work later and swiftly sprays a liquid to get a rich brown tone. A towel is then applied to soak the extra liquid and then a topcoat of lacquer, the paint applied in thin strokes with a soft brush slowly giving a gem-like brilliance to Valentine's skin.

'Can you believe it? Thackray wants me in an action workshop! What the fuck does one do in action workshops—jerk each other off? And where is the condescending prick himself? Where is Mr Legend?' Valentine's voice is full of contempt.

There was a time when Valentine and Thackeray used to be close. They had started their careers by temping in bad two-reelers, him in front of the camera and Thackeray behind it. They would end their days in bars where they would dream of success and getting away from commercial cinema. Young and ambitious, they would imagine spinning genius ideas over a mug of beer with a desperate desire to stun the world. But the friendship had faded away and they were not on good terms anymore.

'I am packing up. I refuse to wait for the legendary bastard—

Binky, who the fuck are you talking to? Did you hear what I said? Dammit man—what happened?'

Binky is pale as a ghost when he says, 'Mr Thackray's body has been found. The police says the body is mutilated...some wild animal had dragged him deep into the forest they think...'

Valentine has stopped listening. His body is quivering like a track just before the train thunders in, a live wire throwing current. A rapid swell of heat inside his head threatens to explode.

'Dead?' Valentine rolls the word on his tongue as if he has just discovered it.

୴

Watching Valentine leave the sets, the thin-faced man restrains a smile. He knows the real reason behind the darkness which lurks around the star's eyes, the redness of his skin and the slight droop of the mouth—a far cry from the Golden God, Valentine once looked like.

10

Este
Monday, 2 November
The Dune

The baby sneezes and rubs its soft thumb on its nose leaving a round nub of redness. Something swells inside Este, a certain warmth which she is still not used to and in confusion she hurries her pace. A car swerves in her direction, blocking her path. Its window is rolled down and young boys, in their twenties, start a conversation. Covering the child with her shawl, she shakes her head, but the boy in the driver's seat makes a crude gesture as if to ask her rate. She gestures with her hands that she is not available. The boys stay put talking to each other and suddenly one of them tries to pull her inside the car. It is not a violent pull, more like a physical coaxing to help her make up her mind, but she wrenches out her hand in an annoyance which does not border on fear yet. A second boy gets out of the car and it is then Este breaks into action. Reaching in her bag she pulls out a mace. The boys slam the doors of their car shut, but not before hurling abuses at her. Este stares back at the receding car with indifference. It's not their fault completely. Every soul walking on the streets of the Dune at any time of the day is for sale. Soon the place will be teeming with night-walkers with their depressing smiles, peddling sensations for a rupee, their souls for lesser. She wants to be home before the place transforms into a hell-hole teeming with murky lives.

Este is seventeen years old and has already mastered the basics of survival in this place. It's all about not hanging outside at the wrong time. There was a time when she would lose her way in the arid squares, and returned home black and soiled and mindless with fear. Not anymore. Immune to the foulness, she almost sprints now through the familiar twists and turns. Her flat is in a dilapidated building which sits fenced in on two sides by a severely pitted rocks and bushes with twisted limbs and pasty poppies spread aimlessly on either side like armies of coked-out crackwhores. She was just five years old when her mother Hiri's first attempt to kill herself failed—by swallowing mercury from a broken thermometer. She narrowly survived but afterwards, neither did she remember her name nor the fact that she has a daughter. Multi-drug abuse has eaten up her brain. Este does not like to leave her mother alone for this long usually, but her uncle has promised he will visit today and she is happy with the extra hand. She wonders if her uncle knows this. He looks the sort who 'knows' things. At times, she feels he can even look inside her head and if it were not for his gentleness she would have found him abnormal. All she wants is that her mother would not go crazy yelling 'Ghost' every time he shows up at the door.

'Ma'rm...?'

The room is too quiet. The sheets are rumpled, the pillows scrunched; the bedroom looks as if it might have been the site of a nightmarish orgy. Hiri looks worse today, all blanched and waxen. She must have sneaked out. Pine needles and leaves are stuck to her soles and her toes scratched on the scaly red and blue-tiled floor.

'What happened, Ma'rm? Did you open the window? Salt ain't good for your skin—'

'Shut your bitch face cunt up, you bitch.'

'Ma'rm, just go to sleep. You will wake up the baby,' Este says and the child starts crying.

'Yaaahhh—your baby? That devil's baby…just like you…devil's spawn…'

'Ma'rm, stop it.'

'A whore you are for keeping your ma'rm locked in this fuck room—arrhhh fuck—I'm hot, too hot, I am boiling—witch, why don't you help your ma'rm?' she blabbers incoherently, 'He is here isn't he? Whore, you can't fool me! The ghost you meet—I know… I see him… I see him…he is coming for me—' Hiri coughs and her voice almost drowns the heavy sound of the motorcycle being parked outside. Este opens the door and smiles back warmly. The man takes the child in his arms and kisses its warm forhead.

'Where is Hiri?' he asks.

Hiri

Her daughter makes her so mad, calling her a coke-head, locking her in and running off, and hiding her in a room as if she is something to be ashamed of. Hiri's heart swells up with special hatred but she is not sure if it is just one person or more whom she should blame. In panic, Hiri stumbles clumsily over a box of old costumes—her wildly flailing arms grabbing the curtains for support but her thin legs fail to support even her fragile weight and they come crashing down adding to the momentum of her fall. She falls flat on her stomach and lies spread-eagled with a gobsmacked expression on her face. Incensed, she stomps childishly on the dusty curtain tearing it to shreds. All of a sudden she becomes restless with a burning urge to fuck. Legs spread out, she clenches a cloth with her hands and stuffs it deep inside her crotch, moving it frenziedly till she is all red and bruised. She takes a blade and makes a sharp cut on her thigh, near her vagina, and shoving her fingers up in the warm wetness she continues jerking till her body releases her with a shudder. Spent, she curls up in a foetal position and the shadows take over.

'Hiri,' the man calls out. His voice terrifies her. A hand taps on her shoulder as she bursts into uncontrollable frenzied screams.

'The—the ghost is here, the ghost... ghost—will get me—help me—'

Hiri's crazed eyes are fixed on a worn-out poster—a beautiful man with soft lips and soft hair woven of sunlight offset by a prominent crooked nose. A young Valentine, looking very much like a shiny Adonis.

1993

In the morning, I noticed it was an abandoned thatch, a pitted ribcage of rotting hay for a roof, its single window blocked with wild nettle and rubble. Weak from hunger, I crouched and waded into the red river, swimming along with the plump lui fish. The water climbed to my thighs and then stomach, my malnourished body was ready to give in. The sand in the waters was full of slippery weed and my wet clothes dragged me down. Cramped arms could do no more and just when I was about to let go, a plump red lui jumped right into my hands. I devoured it raw.

As I rested, my mind shifted to Hiri and the first time we had slept together. Hiri knew what I felt for her, and that evening when I was returning from the bushes with the lime herbs mother wanted for her medicines, I ran into her again. She wanted to show me how horses fuck and led me to the farm-hands. A black stallion was mounting a white mare which was his own offspring. She gripped my hand tightly when the stallion with the help of the farm-hands finally found his way and sank himself into the mare's belly. That night she came into my bed. We were both still excited from what we had witnessed and the next thing I knew my hands were on her breasts. During sex, she kept talking about the new medicine factory. It was almost as if she was fucking someone else. I would have fucked her every night if it hadn't been for the fight which caused tensions in the village.

From my hiding place, I peered down at the long lines of trucks entering and leaving the mountain. The distant factory lights stared back with multiple lidless windows, the painted face of a beast. It was at the medicine factory where I saw Mr Sonny for the first time. He was the manager of the new 'miracle pill' medicine factory which was being built on the richest soil near the red river.

The first time I saw Mr Sonny he was with a bunch of city people. But our eyes were transfixed on a beautiful young man who was a movie actor. We had never seen anyone like him. Hiri called him a young god in human flesh. He had beautiful brown eyes, crooked pearls for teeth and a slightly dented nose and Mr Sonny paraded him around like a prized stallion. Mr Sonny did not own the medicine company but acted like he did and spoke softly as if he did not want to be held by his words. Mother did not trust him or his medicine factory. During the village meeting there was an ugly fight when mother bluntly told Mr Sonny that the factory's 'miracle pill' was a lie as it was simply not possible to cure everyone with one pill. Mr Sonny angrily walked away from the meeting but the next day he got the bank officer and the village headman and announced the handing over of our land to the factory. Mother said the headman had been bought with a hefty percentage. The whole time Mr Sonny was talking about 'draw you a cheque' and 'we can advertise on paper in a day or two' and 'free medicines and jobs for everyone'. Mother called the headman a traitor and Mr Sonny a conman, but the headman said nothing could be done and the factory would be built for the land was sold and we were welcome to leave the village.

I was thinking of all this when a straggly hair touched my leg and my muscles froze snapping link to the nerves of my body. I realized I had stepped into a nest of blueworm maggots which only feed off carcasses. In my haste, I slipped deeper into a crevice and was instantly saddled in a corpse's soggy embrace. I had found my friend, Buddhi.

11

Rathi Thackray
Saturday, 7 November
Dinesh Thackray's bungalow

The red darkness over her closed lids tells Rathi that its way past sunrise. She slowly eases them open giving them time to adjust to the unusually bright day. Last night's uneaten dinner is still on the tray. A stray memory of Valentine fucking her arouses her and she feels guilty thinking of sex when her father has just died.

Rathi's mother had died of brain atrophy while giving birth to her. Her father often joked that she had sucked out her mother's brain, killing her. The thought had terrified her for the longest time. When the other kids teased her about the strange gold and blue specks in her eyes, he convinced her to tell them that it was because a star had burst when she was born and all the light had entered her eyes. She got to know much later that it was actually a pupil deformity, a one in a million chance of getting it unless it ran in the family. Her father never had the conventional fatherly concerns about her stepping into oncoming traffic or accepting candy from strangers or, later on, her ample drug misadventures and rehab trips. When she turned her attention to films he was non-committal and forgot to attend her debut premiere, but had cruelly tweeted: 'Rathi's acting is without passion, but she will earn money.' Rathi never forgave him for the remark but a part of her wondered at the truth of the assessment, for even today at the height of her reasonable success she finds her craft is no more than a means to survive, just a job. He merely texted when he had married an actress half his age, and overnight Rathi had gotten a stepmother. Their last meeting ended in a huge fight—over her dating Valentine. She had scoffed at him for giving 'lessons on morality' and warned him not to interfere in her life.

That had been almost a year ago. And now it is too late to ask questions anymore. Maybe she should have tried hard enough. She should have said something…done something. She longed for a deep sleep so that her mind could go blank. But the Dinesh Thackray in her head refused to rest. Hours later she decides to not give into the grief rushing to swallow her and enters the hall to mourn her dead father, with strangers.

The mourning hall is overflowing with long-stemmed white roses in white pots, white curtains and lots of people in white clothes. A life-size picture on a wall of her grandmother, Mona Thackray, in her youth scrutinizes the guests with her blue and gold speckled eyes. Rathi spots her grandmother soon enough from across the room offering orange juice and gazpacho shots, avocado and butternut squash to the guests. Eyes full of characteristic scorn, Mona moves about in slow motion as if afraid of allowing some final defence to crumble. She is accompanied by her oldest friend and veteran actress, Bela, whose expectant expression is of one waiting for their favourite theatre to start. Though time has erased all traces of beauty from Mona's features and all that remains of a once glorious youth is a wrinkly ball, but the old woman's arrogance has only grown over the years. Like many bitterly arrogant people she firmly believes in social nomenclature, which by birth has placed her on the top of the social pyramid and she is never at ease with those she considers socially inferior to her. Even today Rathi's grandmother is sharply aware of the order of serving and seating arrangements, with the first row at the memorial reserved for the socially elevated.

'My son…my Danny boy…was a creative fanatic, if nothing else. He was voice of the deprived.' Mona's tone betrays the exhaustion of her nerves, 'I think we should remember what he stood for. The talented Bela who had assisted him in several projects will now open our minds to the unconscious world of my son.'

'Dinesh would have hated this stupid Stanislavsky shitness, okay…? Errm that's all I guess. Sorry just…one more thing…minds are like wounds. If you keep them too open, they catch infection. Yeah so let's ditch this conscious and subconscious shit—' Bela pauses mid-sentence. Heads turn to watch a pretty young girl who stands smiling unsurely in the doorway.

Kimmy White might as well have stood there stark naked, such is the affect she has on the gathering and Mona stares in shock. The girl waits a moment to be received or announced, but when nobody makes any gesture of welcome her features harden into a stubborn expression. With her head bowed and her eyes suitably misty, Kimmy has arrived at the funeral service uninvited. She nods at Rathi in a greeting, who can't help but marvel at Kimmy's boldness. While everybody looks on confused, Bela is chuckling as she settles back into her seat.

'Who invited you here? Please leave. You are not welcome.' Mona's eyes are a watery pink, not unlike an albino raven's.

'Calm down, Mona. I don't need an invitation. The divorce still has to come through.' Kimmy said as she looks around the room hoping to exchange a victorious smile but fails to catch anyone's eye.

'The shame of it! We have nothing to do with you. No more free gold wells for your kind to dig around here!' At Mona's words a shadow passes over Kimmy's face like a cloud over the sun.

'You cannot stop me from paying my last respects to *my husband*. The divorce hasn't been finalized yet, didn't the lawyer tell you? Kimmy pretends naively.

'Get out! Go back to the street where you belong. Or I will have you removed physically, you whore.' Curses poured out like soft slush from Mona's mouth. She crumbles on the floor with a thump and Bela has a hard time getting her back on her feet. Rathi wants to recede inside her head. Her father had truly outdone himself in his choice of women. The funeral service broke up into a three-ringed circus. To hell with them. For her, the farce of mourning her father has been hijacked by third-rate comedy.

Rathi begins running. She runs as fast as she can and as far as she can. She runs till her legs lock and she falls. Her body shakes as she holds her head between her hands, and then she begins to laugh. Clutching her stomach, Rathi laughs madly almost as if she were possessed. Tears roll down her cheeks as she doubles up with helpless laughter. She is emotionally exhausted by the time she stops laughing, but is no more numb to feelings or in denial anymore—probably past the first stage of grieving. When she looks up she realizes that she is in a large terrace garden that had been her father's—till he had abandoned it with his typical callousness.

The garden is soaked in a mysterious calmness. When her father was alive the place was strictly off limits to everyone, mostly because of his preferred choice of plants—giant crocus, poppy and hogweed, mandrake and even some cannabis and henbane—a chronicle of the sinister side of the plant world. Rathi finds herself go utterly quiet. Noise, she thinks, would somehow violate her father's memory at a deep level. She moves across towards the large wall mount multi-shelf storage unit filled with old articles, newspaper cuttings and magazines on strange medicinal plants and rare drugs. He was stocking up to rid of the 'pains' was what he said to anyone who complained of the vile smell. But just like everything else in his life, the garden was abruptly abandoned and would have withered and died had Mona not restored it to life. An odd looking plant gets her attention. The way it stands out of the ground something in the soil seems to be impeding its growth.

She takes a gardener's knife and shaves off its decaying leaves. Hidden in its bulbous stems are unusual flowers of a sweet mouldy smell. Like something gone sour, impure. The flowers are starting to turn brown and the roots are partially exposed. Rathi works into the dry cracked soil wondering if the disintegrating plant would survive the invasion. But she cannot let it die like this, trapped in memories of what life was and her spade pushed deeper into the dark composted soil. The soil is ungiving and when she forcefully yanks out the spade she spots the black-polythene wrapping. For the next half hour she straddles the ground in a crab-like manner, peeling away the soiled plastic sheet from a midget-wood case, pitted and cracked. It is a small-sized medicine drawer filled with expired and discarded medicines. Rathi realizes it is a detachable part of the wall mount multi-shelf storage unit. Gingerly extending her fingers to search the interiors, she knocks around with her knuckles undoing a jammed shelf. Running her fingers around the minute area, she discovers that it is empty.

What the hell was she expecting to find here in any case?

Feeling strangely disappointed Rathi decides to leave before Mona came looking for her, when it suddenly dawns on her what she had found odd in the first place.

Why the hell would anyone remove a drawer from a perfectly good wall-to-wall rack? Something is wrong with the fact that it is even there. Rathi goes back to inspect the storage unit with a beam torch trying to recall what else had struck her as odd and plays the torch along the edges. She has almost given up when a faint glint catches her eye. It glints again at the same spot when she moves the torch. Removing the old newspapers from the shelf, she peers inside. And then she sees it for what it is. A hinge placed in an odd position. There is only one reason for it and she finds it soon enough: the hidden compartment. Feeling a sudden beat of excitement she retrieves a thick envelope and sits down on the floor to inspect it. Dusting the grime off the photographs with a free hand she narrows her eyes for a closer inspection.

They are amateurly shot photos of several men, she can make out from their sillouettes, men with their faces hidden; shot against the light. All of them seemed focused on a very young girl, a child, maybe twelve or thirteen, completely naked she realized with growing horror. Rathi was transfixed by the girl's face, a brazen smile, full lips and the pearl white teeth like in an advertisement for dental-cosmetics. The men in the picture were casually groping the girl's breasts and thighs with their fingers—Rathi's first instinct was to look away, but is drawn back to the girl, who seemed unashamed of her nakedness or what the men were doing to her. The photos are old and not very clear and the men were in enough shadow to eclipse their faces. Trapped between the grating and the bottom of the drawer of the cabinet she sees another picture. The light is dim but she can clearly make out a face. Her father's.

In the future, Rathi would remember this moment as when order disappeared forever. Ground into pieces by unstoppable emotions. The room seems sordid and dirty, the birds feral, the fruits evil, the air demonic, the sun malevolent.

She forces herself to look at the picture again. Her father with an unguarded expression on his face, the kind she has never seen before. It revolts her.

At the top right corner of the photo is scrawled a clumsy hand *'roobi bloo'*.

Rathi stumbles into the bathroom and turns up the cold water. Sitting on the edge of the tub her legs curled, head lowered to her knees as she watches the chilled water gush out and hit her. But the pain coming out in gigantic spurts does not stop. A faint ringing begins from somewhere and goes on and on and its constant wail fills her universe, and when she looks up she sees it is coming from her phone. It's an unlisted number. The man identifies himself as Investigating Officer Dorab Silva. He tells her that he is investigating her father's death.

12

Molly Limaye
Monday, 9 November
Press room, Medici Studio

There are no witnesses. No obvious crimes. That's how big companies get away with criminal misconduct or, as in this case, worse. Molly Limaye does not like to pick fights for their own sake. This time what she is dealing with is not some run-of-the-mill fraud or some low-level espionage stuff. She is messing with a powerful and deep-pocketed company. For the past several weeks, she was confronted by an entirely unexplicable event—she had started receiving anonymous packets. The contents baffled her—copies of private correspondence between Medici and a number of companies and personalities and NGOs, photocopies of cheque details, gift vouchers and proofs of purchase exchanges with distinguished NGOs, illustrious doctors, prominent celebrities and their extended representation of Medici, adhoc lobbying subsidiaries names listed in organized detail. She had initially dismissed the whole thing, convinced the packet was delivered to her by mistake. But this morning another anonymous packet had been delivered and a second time could not be dismissed as an aberration. In the little time she had before she rushed to the Medici press conference she managed a rapid inventory check of the contents—photocopies of numerous legal affidavits and property bond listings—some stuff she could not make head or tail of—documents which to her alert senses seemed to suggest a collusion between the Medici and numerous big brands and powerful companies. Deeming her mystery abettor 'X', her astute mind had approached the mystery, as she would a quasi mathematical truth.

1. X has a covert grudge against Medici.
2. X is a competitive pharma company.
3. X is an insider from Medici (though she ruled out some disgruntled store-level employee angst). Definitely not the work of a soul sick of corporate abuse receiving minimum wage—this has to be someone with a deeper grudge against Medici, while feeling alarmed by the nature of the confidential letter.

The Complaint
Ref: GOC and SO vs Medici
Subject: Illegal attempt by Medici to evergreen patent
Court: Regional Court of Pharma Malpractice (RCPM)

'As a responsible body of social organizations, it is our responsibility to bring to urgent notice of the court the disgraceful attempts of Medici Pharmaceutical Company to illegally evergreen its patent right for the Heal drugs. It is a worrisome strategy by certain companies to attempt ever-greening of their patent right for certain medicinal products by attempting to renew the rights to the same by bringing in some very minor changes such as adding new mixtures or formulations or minor variations in terms of absorption values and in effect actually adding nothing of value for the patient. Medici has been engaging in this questionable practice whenever their patent is about to expire. Our worry is

if the patent on Heal is granted, it could give Medici a twenty-year-old monopoly on the drug which is grossly overpriced. A month's dose is around ₹1.2 lakh, much higher than ₹8,000 which is the price of the generic drug.'

The Rebuttal
Ref: Medici vs GOC and SO

'The purpose is not to make money from the poor. This is not the purpose, but are we not entitled for patent for our drug? We are fighting the case on principle. We, the Medici firm completely reject the mischieveous attempts by the individuals heading GOC and SO to create the impression that our new Heal drug has nothing of benefit to offer or that our drugs would be beyond the reach of poor patients. Falsehoods and fabrications are being spread about Heal drug.

'We, at Medici, submit that there should be no cause of concern that the poor would not get treatment and submitted that 85 per cent of the patients are treated free under its scheme. We would like to make it clear that we are going ahead with the launch of our new Heal derivative.'

'We, at Medici, coinciding with the launch of the Heal derivative vaccine, will release Healers the series starring none other than our generous patron and well-known philanthropist Superstar, Mr Neville Valentine who is not charging us a single penny to work in this movie. For he, like the lakhs we have successfully treated, believes in us and is with Medici to spread its message of making healing—'

A commotion signals the hero's arrival. There is a dense, almost impenetrable crowd around Valentine. If Molly were to put the scene on paper, it would say a den of a wizard of such compelling shape, form, and colour that it mesmerized his beholders till they had no choice but to remain captive to his being. No one finds it strange that a single man wielded such extraordinary power over so many.

'Ladies and gentlemen—we take great pride in presenting 'Biocide'—our new Heal drug. This vaccine is a breakthrough treatment drug…' Dr Diaz drones on practically uninterrupted. But Molly is hardly listening. Her gaze is fixed on Valentine. He looks pale and tired. Sleep deprivation does send them hurtling to the finish line faster than any opiate, she thinks.

'Ladies and gentlemen—we at Medici have laid open the womb of nature and revealed many secrets of excellent use that no man has reached before. The point is no longer just to know nature but to conquer and subdue her with the power of science. We will take the fight to its logical conclusion…' Molly moves to raise a question. Valentine stiffens and Dr Diaz firmly ignores her raised hand.

'Ladies and gentlemen, we need to storm the bastions of nature with the tools Medici has perfected. We have isolated the powerful properties of plants, extracted them, and synthesized them into chemicals and drugs. The human body has become the central battlefield and we are at war against diseases. Biocide will bombard the contaminant cells… we have an arsenal of drugs and of "magic bullets" that target all deformity. Thank you for a wonderful session. Before the press conference ends—presenting β-Lui243, a perfectly hermaphrodite redfish created on an entirely Medici treated diet in our lab. It is exceptionally fertile and lays a thousand eggs—a day!' The fish has a bloated mouth and is swimming in a glass round-bottomed flask.

'Hey! You have some nerve! You were NOT invited!'

Molly steps back as an angry Binky moves towards her. She had heard about Binky Mendez and his near pathological loyalty to his boss. Legendarily feral, the man was, at close quarters, harmless to behold. She is aware the man's untidy short crop of hair conceals a mind like a bear trap.

'I am sure you know who I am.'

'The industry version? The one which says that Binky Mendez would burn down your house if you give him a quarter of an excuse and half just for fun? No, I haven't!' she smiles.

'You flatter me. If envy was an acid in that room, there would have been nothing left of Mr Valentine except his teeth and belt buckle. But you do not look impressed,' Binky accuses.

'I am not a conventional fan if that's what you mean.'

'The public loves him.'

'The public also accords acceptance to State-sanctioned whorehouses. I look at it as some outlet for base instincts which have to be provided. I guess—someone has to do this sort of a thing too.' Molly's voice could have cut paper.

'Your editor described you in apt words.'

'What did he say?'

'Hungry, cheap and churns out a copy every second,' Binky retorts.

'A comprehensive assessment, I would say.'

'You are building a case where there is none.'

'Isn't it a fact that a formal complaint has been filed againt Medici at the industrial malpractice court for illegalities in evergreening your Heal drugs?'

'Is there a question in the horizon?'

'Depends on which peak you are gunning for.'

'I look for context.'

'You mean dirt to make byline?'

'It keeps the paper in profit. Our editor has an odd idea that we need to make profit.'

'You interrogate as if someone has committed a crime here! Is this a court trial for some imagined crime of a company which you are fixated on in your head. And you think Mr Neville is supposed to be answering your ridiculous questions?'

'Guilty as charged. I do think too much... but I am a journalist, not a publicist.'

'You should not waste time by running false information.'

'Truth does not need the sanction of your interpretation.'

'You know all you are doing at the end of the day is accusing an artiste of bad commerce.'

'Artiste? Well-compensated perhaps, but critically ignored as far as I can tell. The media, yes, occasionally we love to rub it in.'

'You could lose more than a byline here you know... is it worth it?'

'I'd regret it—are you threatening me?' Molly dismisses the man with a voice as cold as a motel ice machine.

Binky Mendez looks thoughtfully at the redfish trapped in the glass cage.

'So β-Lui243, you turn to soup tonight. Question is, how far will someone go to taste your fillet?'

13

Ranganathan
Monday, 9 November
Better Deal Pharmacy, City Link Road, Exit 3

The Better Deal Pharmacy store, a small chemist on City Link Road, is not crowded at any time of the day, the sole reason why Ranganathan prefers to shop here. But the newly installed CCTV in the store makes him nervous. He does not want the CCTV camera to catch his front profile when he pays for the condom packet. You never know who might be watching. The condoms are a necessary precaution. With the boys one never knows who all they've been with and what they might be infected with. He doesn't want to risk an infection at his age. Ending up senile at a farm holding a dry dick is one of his persistent worries.

But the new boy is a treasure house of delights with soft lips and the tightest brown ass. In his arms, the boy felt like he weighed only a few grams. Like a bird. There was something about the boy's lightness against his heaviness that made him want to devour him whole. Giddy, he shut his eyes. Last night the boy just wouldn't stop crying. Ranga called it 'toughening up' and had to scold him. But the boy was crying so much that finally Ranga had to feed him strong pills to dull the pain. Ranganathan does not like drugs—weed slows them down, coke drives them to a frenzy and stoked pills are the worst, after a point it's like fucking a cadaver. No fun.

There was a time when he liked their first rush of panic the most, taming them gave him a high. Now he prefers them eager and willing. He does not have the energy to use force. Ranga does not feel bad for the little boy; he should have known there is nothing like a free hot meal. Shrewd little bastard probably wants to snuff out more money from him. The boy was not going anywhere, the pills will ensure that. But before any of that, there is business to be taken care of.

14

Aslam Kapadia
Friday, 13 November
Medici Studio

Aslam Kapadia had joined the film industry to become famous and he is grateful that Allah had granted his most fervent wish. With Thackray dead, he is now the 'lead director' of *Healers*. But the problem is that Aslam, in just a few days of being on his own, is, as they say, stuck at first base.

'Get off my frame, idiot—don't play whore and fuck the wall, do your thing—JUMP—JUMP DOWN—,' Aslam's voice cracks with a stifled intensity. His impatience is directed at Stud the stuntman stuck on the fake wall, a surreal speck of black against a pink sky. Aslam wants Stud to jump off the wall for a perfect shot but the petrified stuntman refuses to budge.

'Stud won't move. Not without a strap-harness—' an assistant director confirms.

'So? Are you not a production controller, douchenozzle? Go control.'

'We don't have the harness. You refused the budget. Stud says he is scared he might die. I think we should get the professional harnesses to reduce the risk—'

'Just handle the shit—I am a creative guy, this is not my fucking department—' Aslam's high-pitched yell is like a shotgun blast in the air. By now the production unit is aware that Aslam's creative process is akin to dropping an egg on the floor. The momentary suspension of time just after the shell cracks and spits out the yolk, sticky and messy and no one knows whether to clean it up or just walk around it. And suddenly all you want is to be done with it.

※

'So, with the sad development of Mr Thackray being no more, the ball is, as they say, firmly in your court, mister!' Ranganathan settles down with an air of expecting only good news. That's when Aslam sees Kimmy White.

'Why is she here?'

'Where else would she be, mister? She is a part of *Healers* now. We want you to amplify her role in the show,' the lawyer and the girl exchange a private look.

'Amplify her role? What for?'

'We think Miss Kimmy White's character will be a better whore if we give her prominence—a whore who turns a new leaf—gets 'healed'…if you know what I mean!'

'Listen here—'

'This film is what I have been born to do—' Kimmy's exaggeration could easily have been taken for a bogus if one doubted her truthfulness. Or empathize with, if one got taken in by her voluptuous beauty.

'An artiste is never happy answering to businessmen!' Kimmy's earnestness could only be matched by the desperate child who doesn't want to be thrown out of her favourite game. Aslam wants to bayonet her mouth.

'We have to be sure the show is imbibed with the beliefs of Medici—peace, non-pollution, healing and sustainable development. And no fucking with our commerce. So, when can we see the script of the final scene of the *Healers*?'

Aslam looks as if the demand for a script was blatantly illegal. He is still deciding on whether to take offence or not at the demand when there was a loud bang followed by a commotion.

'Stud jumped—broke, a bone I think', informs an assistant director.

'Medici will not be responsible for any medical or legal issues—' Ranganathan says with annoyance, 'In any case I had come to inform you that Medici's new executive producer is on the way. The sooner you have this place in order the better for all of us.'

Ranga's words signal a temporary end to the confrontation. Aslam knows he has a few hours to sort out his shit. He hopes the new executive producer does not interfere too much in his creative process.

15

Dorab Silva
Friday, 13 November
City Link Road, Exit 11
Case no. 55/63/2018/dineshthackray/

'You made it, boss?—' Junior Inspector Gouda is surprised to see Silva at work on his day off. He is not sure if it implies that his boss is returning to normalcy. But he keeps his thoughts to himself. 'If you are asking me if I am in shape to handle work then, yes. I am. Still got to have that operation—doc says the disc needs to be replaced—but otherwise I am fine, thank you.' The lacerated evening sun morphs Silva's face into a bronze mask.

'I merely asked as you are still on medication—'

'You look like horseshit yourself.' Silva navigates the car through a wave of car roofs fitted into each other like an blast of metal.

'Always fun talking to you, boss.'

Silva is non-responsive as he recalls the newspaper headlines. They had been predictable:

> MURDER OR ACCIDENT?
> WAS DEPRESSION THE CULPRIT?
> JUMPED OR PUSHED?
> POLICE STILL CLUELESS

And his favourite:

LAW CAUGHT NAPPING

'Do you think Miss Thackray told us everything? I don't trust her.' Silva is troubled by what Rathi Thackray could have chosen not to reveal. She looked the sort who could keep secrets.

'The daughter? She is no nun. The glossies have colourful stories of her affair with Valentine—who in the meantime is also fucking her 'stepmother' if you go by what has been published—and he is old enough to be a father to both of them!' Gouda says rolling his eyes.

'Shut up, Gouda! Her personal life is not under investigation. Yet. But I admit there is something off about her.'

'What do you expect, boss? Her father was a certified pervert! You should have seen her face when we showed her this...' Gouda holds up a picture of an artificial rubber phallus.

'The big gun was shooting empty bullets?' Silva says.

'Or maybe no bullets at all. Perhaps attempted to compensate for his lack of potency? But whoever killed this pervert did him a favour if you ask me, bloody meth-doped bag of bones.' Gouda is emphatic.

'The thing is someone cleaned out his drug cabinet. But we couldn't find any prescription pad. A pill popping juice-head like him must have kept the friendly neighbourhood candyman busy. And there is talk about him having been involved in that fetish club—some FetLife—and the daughter says she had no idea daddy was a closet pervert. Bullshit.' Gouda is as blunt as a knife.

She had no idea—the words hang in the air and Silva feels depressed. He could have taken the day off but the thought of spending time at his lonely house had been disagreeable. Since his wife's death time had refused to budge from the point of the climactic event.

He finds himself thinking of his dead wife. *She looks cheap*—his mother had said, and he had gotten angry with her. He himself had never fully understood his love for his wife. The love which was equal parts of lust and intrigue. The lust part he understood the intrigue part he thought he did. She never really knew the extent of his physical attraction towards her, and believed it to be more of a soulmate connection. But he knew that he'd felt things below his belt before he had felt anything in his heart. When he had proposed to her on a lark, she had been standing on the boat with the sun going down behind her. She was just out of the water, her grey bikini dripping wet at the corners. She had said yes and he had been smiling due to an embarrassing boner that just wouldn't quit. He didn't know then that she was a junkie crack-head—hopelessly addicted to substances. But would knowing about it had changed anything? He had no idea.

'The family almost never ever knows,' Silva is immersed in a cloud of nicotine, 'You sure this woman we are meeting—this Mina Meh—is she legit?'

'Boss, it took the boys a few days but the information is legitimate. Several narcs and a few old timers recognized her. They swear our mystery girl always hung around with this Mina Meh.'

'A whole day and a half just for Ms Meh. She better be worth it Gouda.'

'Boss, didn't I tell you? Miss Meh in her hey days was the highlights of the same club—FetLife. I heard from a bird she was in for raping a minor, talk about FetLife. It's an underground—hugely popular social networking site for BDSM participants. Lists more than 41,000 kinksters living in the cities.'

'Names—?'

'Not likely. It's a secret sect. Quite a few fancy people are members. The whole spanking horse, padded bondage tables sex sling routine. I had another case...the victim had this strange fetish.. self mutilation...similar ones on this woman.' Gouda says.

'Not a woman. A child. Just a child.' Silva sounds tense.

'I think the daughter is lying. How can she not have had a clue?'

'Story of every criminal's family—always the last to know.' Driving in a sullen silence Silva finds his mind wandering off.

Family fucks you the most—
Family gets fucked the most!

Since his wife's death in a road accident, all his 'well-meaning' relatives have been talking behind him in hushed tones and using his dead wife as an example for careless driving. The same relatives also expect him to move on in life now that it has been three years since. She never liked his job. But he had thought he would make her come around. He had thought he had time. They had time. He hadn't expected to become a widower at the age of thirty-six. So what if the woman he had loved was a pothead druggie? When you are that age, death eventualities are the last things on your mind.

'Mind that curve...hey, boss...are you okay? You are giving me your thousand-yard stare ag—' Gouda is still speaking when another vehicle bursts out on the road on the blind side of the curve. A jeep splashed with mud on both sides, its motor roaring like it was pissed off about something changes direction suddenly and heads straight for them. The police car swerves and fish-tails blowing blue grey thick smoke and there is a hideous metallic grinding as Silva up-shifts the gears trying to take the car from zero to 70 in maybe five seconds and their car comes to rest inches from a massive tree. The jeep's mud-caked tail-lights come on and there is a demonic howling as the badly used breaks locked the tires and it disappears in a fuming cloud of black dust. The acrid smell of oil, thick burning fuel hangs in the still air. Silva feels his heart has stopped dead in his chest. Gouda's face is chalky white from the near escape.

'That was close. Got his number?' Silva inspects the car for trauma.

'Yes. But it was not only his fault boss.'

'Well then I hope he did not get our number. Get in the car.'

'Let me drive Boss.'

'Just fucking get in Gouda!'

'Boss. Let me put it this way. I want to have a shot at increasing my retirement benefits. And for that I have to stay alive.'

'Shut up. Fucker.'

'Just let me drive old man,' he says. Silva gives in and settles in the back seat with a wet towel wrapped on his face. The rest of the trip is passed with the men immersed in a cloud of joyless silence intent on carrying out their duty with grim determination. Crossing rusty double wide roads blind alleys balding front yards crusty old men unpleasant dogs lidless plastic tin furniture garbage bins shitting kids and lazy women lying with their heads in the crook of their arms dreaming of the days adventures till, with Gouda at the wheels, it is all a continum whizz of olive and ochre ordinariness. Quite a few crumbling studios and fading cheapie hotels later they reach the far-flung Moonbeam studios off exit seven on the link road.

16

Friday, 13 November
Case no. 55/63/2018/dineshthackray/

MINA MEH
Moonbeam Studio, City Link Road, Exit 7

A unit canteen boy arranges the plates and pots with particular attention with his back very straight, aware that he is serving police officers. Tired and dusty and truly hungry, Gouda nods approvingly at the attention. Beaming from ear to ear with an oily smile, Mr Cheddy, the production coordinator of the set insists on shaking Silva's hand and lets him know with a wink that the lady in question, Mina Meh, would be 'made available' for questioning right after a 'crucial' scene of the film.

'Please enjoy the show, officers,' Mr Cheddy says with a wink which could have meant anything. Silva recognizes Mr Cheddy as the sort who comes to the city for two goals—one to make money and second to treble it.

The hero of Cheddy's film was a balding hulk with a slight belly. A ridiculous wig takes care of the pate, but it is difficult to hide the paunch. On the makeshift stage a skinny dark girl, dressed in third-rate wedding cake style gown, is going over her scene with the producer waving his hand and talking at the top of his voice. The lone cameraman looks bored and sleepy.

'This is depressing,' Gouda declares.

'This is as good as this will ever get.' With Cheddy's imagination helming the tawdry affair, Silva doesn't expect much. The music begins and the dancers in shiny bright costumes with their coarse movements try their best to emote creatures of the finer world. They come across as unbelievably wanting. The self-contained lead actress, pretty in an obvious way, speaks with too much passion, her gestures ridiculously artificial, she is over-emphasizing every dialogue as if they hold no real meaning to her.

> *'You beautiful man, take me... take me!'*
> *'My love... my love, take my hand... I will take you to the other world—'*

If the staginess of the acting makes him cringe, the accidental humour forces a smile out of him. The act has a bizzare appeal. Much like a deformed child who insists on running the race. At that point Mina Meh enters with assorted smells of her intoxication and excesses. Wearing golden shorts and bustiers, Mina sits in an amorphous silence seemingly indifferent to the presence of the policemen.

'It's imitation,' she clarifies in her stage voice when she catches Gouda staring at her massive neckpiece. 'I am the lead heroine. Everybody can be replaced, but me. These other girls around are only fillers. They call only me when they want a lead heroine for a Chinese or Japanese character.' She declares self-importantly.

In the white light Mina looks diminished and though the woman will not be middle-aged until well into the next century, but Gouda's initial idea that she was a beauty queen takes a hit. He guessed her to be in late thirties, but adds two more years when he sees the dark age spots on the thinning skin under her eyes.

'You watched my shooting? What do you think?' She asks a

little too loudly.

'You were...emphatic,' Silva says.

'This is a full-length feature film. Loaded with sex scenes, murders and rapes. Am I in trouble?' her pitch drops two levels to almost casually intimate as if she is confiding to an old friend and not being questioned by a sceptical policeman.

'Should you be?'

Mina looks up warily. Her eyes glitter with a slyness Silva has often seen in delinquents pretending to be pups. And who have been told they are entitled to lesser punishment than they deserve.

'Mr Cheddy will throw me out,' she mutters childishly.

'Why will Mr Cheddy throw you out, Miss Meh?'

'Because it's easy to find someone else if they think I've fucked up. No one likes policemen visiting.'

'Let's not waste time then. Where do I find her?' Silva pushes the picture in front of her. Mina opens her mouth and then closes it only to open it again like a fish gasping for air. And then she shuts up as if she has decided not to implicate herself by divulging any information. At least not before she has heard what the policeman have to say to her.

'No, I am not familiar with that face—' she says in a thin voice and pushes the picture away.

'Are you sure? Because we have information which indicates otherwise.' Silva puts down his glass of brandy, cracks his knucles in an intimidating way and pushes the picture back to her. Silva realizes that the woman's cognac eyes are actually contact lenses.

'Do you know, Miss Mina, one becomes bound to what one says in front of a police officer? Bound to the repercussions of what you say—truth or lie—and if you lie you have to keep on lying and compound it with smaller lies—getting caught in the chain reaction of your own lazy mistake. You don't want to face the fallout.' There is an unsettled quality in the way he spoke. It was both provoking and safe, and Mina is undecided on whether to trust him or not.

'There is always a fallout.' Gouda nods his head ominously.

'Before you say anything. We have more pictures—of this girl and you and some more with a man who is unfortunately dead now. You know which dead man am I talking about? Mr Thackray's death is much in news—a girl is missing, a man is dead. And you are with them in some pictures. That's enough ground to call you to the station.'

'How are you sure I know her? Maybe this girl was a fan who had a picture taken with me...' There were strains of panic in her voice.

'We also have pictures of the two of you with the dead man behaving as more than mere fans!' Silva takes a gamble on a hunch. Mina Meh frowns and bites her lip.

'Photos are the last thing you can trust here. Anything can be morphed these days,' she said.

'Sure, technology can do magic. Just the other day I saw Mandela snapped with Hitler, looked the real deal I swear. But there's a senior chap who's been in the business longer than you've lived—he says yours are authentic.'

'I have nothing to do with it.' Cheery and effusive has become distrustful.

'Never said you had. Did I say so? Ask your friends here! Many vouch for the fact that you knew her well. And a man is dead now.'

'Look everyone knows everyone here. No crime in knowing people. It's a small world,' she said in a weak voice.

'As soon as you tell me about this girl, it will also be a better world.'

'Hmmm...fine. Let me take a look... I could not place her

before…but now that I think…she looks like a girl I knew… I think her name was Hiri or something. But wait it could very well be Este too…Hiri's daughter. The kid had taken after her mother. Wait…this looks like an old photo—it has got to be that old bitch. Oh yes, it's Hiri all right—those mocking cat-like eyes as if she was better than all of us. She always thought of herself as someone special, as if she came from some magical place…what a hoot! Always tripping on coke and talking of her golden-faced prince. Absolutely nuts, if you ask me. She was a troublemaker, they even threw her out of the swish set…'

'The swish set? What do you mean?' Silva enquires.

'Girls picked for important men—FetLife. Don't tell me you havn't heard of it! Rich men, businessmen, corporate types, famous actors—just rich people with lots of money than they know what to do with—you know, the important types,' She explains.

'Important types? People like Thackray?'

'Yeah maybe—look—no one uses real names in the club in any case, most were anonymous profiles. So, I can't say for sure. It's a fishing ground. Users were identified by their sexual tastes, post photos of their bruises and rope marks, and narrowed down potential partners by fetish, searching for things like caging and confinement, clamps and clips, nun and priest play, or a standard flogging—'

'You both were members for long?' Silva probes.

'She was in it longer than me, that I can say for sure.'

'You stopped being a member?'

'Yes, you can say that.'

'Why? Not happy with the pay?'

'No, officer. I didn't like the hours.'

'What about other girls? Anyone else you remember she would hang out with?'

'Look. It was not like we had a union or something. And no one was there to make friends. I experimented a bit, but freaked out. Not my scene, officer, I love my skin too much. But she majored in it. Don't know who got her in. Never talked about it. Initially, she got to go to the best parties, had the best money—always swimming with A grade stash—was crazy though. The most exciting men were the ones who beat her up.'

Silva knew that kind of women. Their tastes verged on the sadomasochistic and with passing years they required increased doses of the shock treatment provided by men.

'That's all I can tell you,' her tone is flat and tired.

'Is that all you know?'

'She was a doped-out crackhead—fizzed out in the head seeing monsters in the day—made a scene one day looking for her kid, Este—turned out her little Este was pregnant—had a bun in her oven! Hiri made a huge fuss screeching and shouting. No one has time here for such family shit. I don't know more—you could find her at the Dune,' Mina Meh says while getting up.

'Fine. I will take your word for now. But what are these marks on your legs? They say it hurts when you get them done.'

Her slanted eyes were tiny slits as Mina Meh got up from her chair. 'I am an artiste. An actress. You have to be one here in this city to know what it's like when you are a nobody. But I am no whore. At least no more than most women or men. Love doesn't pay bills, unless you're a prostitute with no talent. You know, its called the valley of the beautiful—the Dune. That's where the rich keep the ones they are ashamed of.' Mina Meh walks away with a strange pride adjusting the huge feathered hat on her head.

'What do you think, boss?' asks Gouda.

'What's to think? Let's go. To the valley of the beautiful.'

17

Friday, 13 November
Case no. 55/63/2018/dineshthackray/

Girl X
The Dune

The Dune defies all description of ugliness. It jiggles and swells to its own vile sounds and intoxicating smells under a sky of a hideous yellow cast like nature had shat into it. Zinc roofs with water leaking through rusted streets taking a piss on themselves, brown crusted shit, drying semen, used condoms on pavements infested by damaged men. An ugliness of such a mind-numbing range that it was impossible not to stare back after taking your eyes off it in disgust. Mina Meh's directions to the sex shop, a favourite of FetLife junkies were bang on. Business seemed to be booming at the sex shop. A newly installed garish neon bulb lit frontage decked with explicit posters and bold mannequins advertised the full range of services extended, including 'way beyond twisted fetishes'. Under its neon roof, a group of girls and boys with hard eyes conducted their business with mannerisms of those bound by an iron clad fate. They were the 'specialists' who catered to a mind-numbing range of fetishes and offered services along with sex toys including 'male masturbators' to 'rechargeable vibrators', 'ultra soft dildos for beginners' to 'flared suction cup base for handsfree' and the latest 'Bluetooth remote control bullet vibrator'. The streets were filled with an organized complex of small strip clubs fronted as all-night bars. Out in front of every door, thin girls in variations of tiny bikinis and cheetah-print heels clutching cheap plastic purses swayed and called out.

'Wooohooohooo!' whores shout as they stroke each others' backs.

'We go have sex! You boys get to watch! How much you pay?'

Gouda looks in their direction, 'Look at this lot. Conceived, no doubt, in the backseat of cars or a pick-up trucks…'

There is a sudden commotion at the sex shop. An ugly physical fight has broken out between two women over money.

'Heiiikkkkk—what's going on?' Gouda hollers and has to physically separate the angry women from clawing each others eyes out. The womens' fury defuses at the sight of the men in uniform. The girl with the Far-Eastern features and a skinny frame is bleeding from the lips. Her assaulter, a portly and mean-eyed woman looks as indignant as a creditor who has failed to collect.

'So—who is the pimp and who is the whore?' Gouda roars. This simple question prompts the skinny girl to launch into her version of the events interspaced by a verbal tirade against her oppressor but the matter is complicated by the girl's propensity to launch into her native language. The men suspect that an overuse of substances has severely meddled with her general sense of recollection.

'Where do we find her?' Cutting through the commotion, Silva thrusts the photograph in front of the thin girl. She stares at it for some time and then a smirk passes her face, but the next moment her features sour into a blank expression. Gouda sighs.

'Listen, if you want to avoid time for whoring and other charges you cannot even dream of right now, you answer the boss,' Gouda said 'Boss' with his fingers moving in a little arc that clearly refers to the whole town at large.

'So, open your gobs or it's jail for you with so many charges that if you ever even come out of it…you will come looking worse than a clown. Even that garbage scum over there will not have a go at you!'

He stresses the force of his intention by jabbing his fingers at a beggar nearby who is scrounging through garbage looking for food or anything useful. The beggar begins to clean the dirt from beneath his finger nails and pulling out little balls of dirt which he put in his mouth and limps towards the men. Gouda would have shooed him away had Silva not stopped him. The beggar holds out his hand as if asking for a trade-off, money for information, but he surprises the policemen when he plonks himself in the backseat of the police car and declares, 'Will take you to her—will take—you to girl X. Let's go to Roobi Bloo, the best fuck-house in the Dune,' he says and winks.

Este
The Dune

She did not look like she had sold her soul to Satan—that is the first thought which comes to Silva when he sees Este. She is standing outside a broken ATM vestibule, under a street light with a small bundle in her hand. Silva observes that she isn't dressed provocatively. Nor does she appear to be on substances. She could have been taken for a working girl waiting for a cab, had it not been for the place she was standing in. The bundle in her arm moves and he realizes she is holding a baby. The closer she gets, the prettier she turns out to be. Slender, golden-skinned the girl strikes him as a natural beauty, and that makes him feel sad.

Her gaze is straight and direct, and for some reason Silva's heart hammers in a strange fashion in his chest as she walks towards them.

'You looking for me? I am Este.'

'You knew we were coming?'

'Word travels fast here.'

'Then you know why we are here?

'When you have been out on these streets as long you'd know the Devil too.' For some reason, he wants to believe her.

'Can you get in the car... I mean we need to talk to you—'

'I would rather we talk here. I don't go with policemen unless they are paying, which is almost never the case,' she states simply. 'Besides my house is nearby.'

'It's fine with me if it's fine with you, Este, standing out here like this. But it may take long and your baby looks cold,' Silva finds himself talking as if he was asking a girl out on a date. Gouda snorts from inside the car.

'She will be fine,' Este said as she snuggles the sleeping baby, 'I just wanted to buy some ice cream for my mar'm. She gets very hot...'

'Let's go around the corner and talk, there is an ice cream place there—I will buy you one,' Silva offers.

'Like a date?' Este winks.

'Sure. All Boy Scouts and Girl Guides here!' Silva said and Gouda snorts louder.

'What about him?' she frowns finally noticing Gouda.

'Don't go by his face. He is actually a nice man. He will sit quietly in the back.' Gouda clambers into the back seat looking sullen.

'Are you not scared being out at this hour?' Silva asks.

'Scared? No. Scared of whom? Policemen like you?'

'Them too.'

'Scared? No. Repelled? Yes. Specially when men think it's okay to cop a feel on cold nights and expect me to be grateful as if I am being felt up by God. They don't even pay. Been robbed. Been raped. Been beaten. Of course I am scared too sometimes. Who wouldn't be? There is always some man trying to take control over. I am fine with it as long as I get paid. The only one with the right to fuck me for free is God. And he has fucked me in more ways than one. But you seem different from the others…'

'Okay, let's go on that date then.'

Gouda rolls his eyes. Este picks a vanilla brick and a pistachio cone.

'So, you know why we are here?' Silva wants to know.

'Well, they told me two policemen have been looking for a particular woman. I thought I might get paid for talking,' she adds in a soft, halting voice. 'I don't want trouble. I have a baby to take care of.'

'And a mother too?'

'Mar'm? Sure, yes. Am I in trouble?'

'For talking to us? No.'

'I have been out on the streets long enough to be able to smell meanness. You are not mean.' Este's voice trails into a shivery silence.

'How old are you really?' Silva asks.

'Old enough to know my situation,' she chides and burst into loud peals of laughter when her baby caught hold of her cheek with its plump fingers. The child gazes at Silva with clear, unafraid eyes. He is struck by their unusualness.

'Her eyes are—unusual—I mean different from yours,' he says.

'I know what you mean. She got her eyes from her father…'

'Is he around?' There is no way to put it delicately.

'No, her father is dead,' she said with a smile. He does not prod.

'Akchheeee! Damn Kaayi, you shit on my dress!' Este exclaims as she removes a handkerchief from her pocket. The child purses its lips into a surprised 'o'.

'It's their skin that stuns me,' she said changing the topic, 'so fine and perfect. Life has not yet dented Kaayi.'

'That's an unusual name. What does it mean?'

'Her uncle named her. So, what did you want to ask me?' she cuts him off abruptly.

'I wanted to ask you about this—girl.' Silva shoves the photograph towards her. The stillness of her expression and her mysterious silence seems an exhortation in its stifled intensity or perhaps a result of deep exhaustion.

'What about her? She has not been a girl for a long time.' She notices Silva's baffled look and explains. 'That's my ma'rm. When she was young of course. I look a lot like her, people say. It's the way the light falls on our faces—my uncle says—but yes that's her.'

'That's your ma'rm? Your mother? She lives here?'

'Lives? She is hardly alive.'

'What does that mean?'

'It means exactly that. She is barely alive. As good as dead. Ma'rm…my mother…she is not well in her head. It's all blurred up here.' She said pointing to her temples.

'How do you mean?'

'Look I will take you to her, if you like. You can see Mar'm for yourself,' she says and swiftly walks to the nearby street.

'Yes, we would like to visit your ma'rm.'

Silva lunges after her, fearful that he might lose her in the confusing geography. Gouda follows in sullen silence.

'Is it far where you live? Do you have anyone else in your family apart from your mother?' Silva asks but Este responds only by walking faster.

The place is not as near as Este had suggested and they end

up walking towards the coast for about a mile. The men follow Este into a dimly-lit tavern, its bright tones of ruby-red and cobalt blue ludicrously stand out against grunginess of the establishment with a board announcing its name as Roobi Bloo, a jam-packed drinkery, its tacky glow-signboard blacked out from outage. The men have to penguin shuffle sideways into the narrow street which opens into rows of tiny rooms with low corrugated tin roof ceilings covered in thick blue plastic material. In its secluded corridors there are bare lightbulbs, ceiling fans, wooden coat hooks, plastic buckets.

'She is inside…my ma'rm, Hiri.'

Hiri

The room smells of long dead happiness and dreams. There is a glimmer of flesh in the back of the room, a half-lit greyish space. Fragile, hollow-cheeked and jawbone stretched to a high point made her teeth almost visible under the stretched membrane of the skin, but even under all that the resemblance between Hiri and Este is striking. The well-worn acrylic upholstery of the chair Este pulls out for him feels scratchy against his skin and Silva almost recoils from the touch of the mouldy padding. Propping herself up on a pile of pillows, Hiri devours the ice cream and though she doesn't speak a word till she finishes it she regards him with such contempt that he is surprised at a whore giving him such a look.

'Leave me alone! Why are you following me?' Hiri pulls the cotton coverlet closer to her thin chest as she hisses, 'who is this dog turd you got, you whore?'

'Ma'rm, it's the policemen.'

Hiri tries to hide a mound of what looks like photos and posters. She shoots out a sore-covered arm to hide them but relaxes when she realizes the cops have no intention of taking away her treasure.

'Isn't she the hussy you looking for? There's nothing to see in me!' Hiri said in a thick tone.

'Ma'rm, he doesn't want to—'

'Shut your bitch face.'

His eyes now adjusted to the dark, Silva notices the glossy posters of several film stars. Infact all the posters are actually of the same man. Neville Valentine. He sighs internally.

'Stop looking at him, he is mine!' Hiri's voice is thick with a mad grip of some dimming pile of nostalgia.

'It's just a poster, Ma'rm. And these are cops.'

'Shut up! All the same—for a piece of tail—will come anywhere! So is this trollop doing you for free? Must be free, this whore gets the free ones here—hey! What you looking at, yellow dog?'

'Damn Ma'rm, that's some real cold shit.'

'Why have you come here—dog turd, you been stickin' your rough cock into that snatch you then do it somewhere else—it's so cold here and you earning so much money—why can't you get me a heater for my bones they been shattering in the cold…' oblivious to the sweltering heat in the room roasting her skin, Hiri screams about being cold.

'Mother, its' hot here and you don't need a heater!'

'This dog shit pervert been staring at me—but does my slutty daughter care? No, she don't…' Hiri hisses scratching the angry heat velts on her skin. Silva has seen enough of her kind before, opiated out souls on a one-way ticket to hell.

'You cop? The ghost tries to get in from the hole—there—he

will get me! Save me cop—you are after me too bast'rd—?' Hiri points at the window muttering to herself.

'It's no one, Ma'rm. No one is after you. NOT the ghost. NOT the policeman. NOT any man. It's in your head,' Este spoke in an unexpectedly loud way, causing Hiri to wail in a bloodcurdling voice.

'Whoring bitch get out aaaaaikkkkthooo—'

'She is getting worse. She cries when she is kept in the shade. She complains of being cold in her bones all the time,' Este said when they reached his car. 'Will you come again?' the question is put softly, followed by a pause.

He feels curiously excited. The girl's eyes bore into his back ones and he supresses the odd lurch in his heart. Silva wonders if she knows what he wants. That he wants to feel her soft hands stroking and caressing him. That he was wondering how her skin would taste and her hair would smell. He turns to look back. She is still standing in the soft shadows under a tall electrical pole, looking tired, drawn.

'Did you see the marks on her body? Seems to have gone the whole yard complete with hook suspensions, rig marks and all that—the marks were very old. Must be from when she was young. Old coot sure looked like a FetLife veteran,' Gouda is always ready to fix a premise and strengthen his case.

Draining ice cold water into his dry throat, Silva is gripped by a maddening frustration. He feels he is missing out on a connection somewhere. As if he had scribbled some important words and try as he might he could not recall why he had written those words in the first place.

18

Rathi and Valentine
Friday, 13 November
Basement cellar, 555 Neverland

Valentine's eyes are fixed at Rathi's crotch where the taut material of her panties have dug into her and outlined the pouty lips. He hooks his thumb beneath the elastic and pulls the fabric down. A puff of curly black hair and the crimson head of her vagina peek out. They move together and gradually their tempo rises, and her hands pull him into her with deeper intensity—she is like an angry machine coaxing every last ounce of power from him. The great climactic sex leads her to a mental blank and for a brief while there was no pain in her head. But Rathi knows that the euphoria will subside when the sated senses and the exhausted body will no longer be able to keep the pain from seeping right back in. Just as she knows that she will be back to wondering if the passion she shares with Valentine is any more significant than the comfort felt amongst strangers sharing a train-berth for a night. She does not mind that he gets up the instant he is satisfied.

'It is better with the meth.' He is callous and void of emotions, and strangely she does not mind the remark. Perhaps constant betrayals have made her less sensitive to punishment cues, to her own humiliation. Or perhaps his lack of empathy for anyone but himself finds a curious resonance with her lack of guilt. But who is she to pass judgement over his lack of scruples; or play arbiter on his character? Wasn't she guilty as well of letting passion score over morals! The man had slept with her 'stepmother' for god's sake!

Just like her father.

'It's hard for me to hate him—am I a freak?' she wonders.

'It's strange to look at you and see Dinesh...' Valentine touches her eyes, but she moves away.

'What we consider beautiful is a dreadful disease, an abnormality—malignant melanoma of the iris—a genetic thing. It's as if the eyes were not sure whether they wanted to be blue or ash-coloured and two stubborn genes—both won't give up, the end result being passed on from mother to son... and in my case, from father to daughter. He used to say some dregs sifted through missing generations and showed up here. Chances of having this is one in a million, unless the abnormality runs in the family. I am scared that he may have passed on more maladies to me which will surface perhaps later or not at all.'

'The young give the family too much importance. My mother, not exactly a beacon of any goodness—with or without her maladies I live happily,' Valentine muses.

'He scared me sometimes—like he wanted to tell me something...'

'Probably that I am a bad man. Maybe he knew how bad I truly am.'

Valentine's look shuts Rathi out. She wonders if his passion is an act and realizes that since the day she saw the damning photographs everything has become fraught with sordid implications. But she is thankful there's no rush of sadness bursting through her like a ripe tomato which is a good sign. And she has enjoyed sex with him today so she must have crossed stage three of mourning. But soon she will have to look for answers. Discreet inquiries had revealed there did exist at the Dune, Roobi Bloo—a debauched hellhole which teems with dubious characters and all things illegal. Had the police officer suspected she was hiding evidence…?

Ma'am, are you sure? Anything at all?

No, there was nothing else, officer.

Perhaps there was something more to her act of 'hiding' Roobi Bloo from the policemen. Maybe a perverted sense of family honour? Perhaps she is more like her grandmother than she thinks.

A chilly wind hits her face in energetic gusts. Someone she cannot see is standing right in front of her and breathing into her face, she imagines, a big bad wolf huffing and puffing outside the house of the little pigs.

It is sitting there.

And she is ready.

'Just this once.' She takes a deep snort and pushes her head back to let the mixture travel down the throat and leaves her body thrumming. He had said it was diluted, but she is not so sure. Valentine spreads the meth mix on her erect breasts and starts licking her so ferociously she wonders if he would eat her alive.

Neither of them notice Kimmy White's angry, white face behind the open bedroom window. Her mouth tightly shut and steely-eyed, Kimmy stood with her hands clawing at a sleek megapixel camera phone with manual focus and extended infrared stabilizer to produce HD images. Ranganathan had warned her that the evidence should be clear. She is satisfied with her work, for the camera works exceptionally well in the dark.

19

Molly Limaye
Friday, 13 November
Apartment No. 503, Glengate (Molly Limaye's Building)

Molly Limaye's head is spinning. But it has absolutely nothing to do with Binky Mendez's strict warning to stay away from Valentine. Because if the contents of the last two unnamed packets had left her intrigued, the latest installments had her alarmed considerably. In a rising state of panic, she rereads the photocopy of the latest complaint against Medici.

> *The Complaint*
> *National Vaccine Information Centre (NVIC)*
> *Ref: GOC and SO vs Medici*
>
> *Subject: Illegal attempt by Medici to evergreen patent*
>
> *Court: (RCIM) Regional Court of Industrial Malpractice*
>
> *'If Medici is able to convince the state to consider giving drug companies partial liability protection through the creation of the new 'vaccine/drug injury compensation alternative' to a lawsuit then language should be written into the National Vaccine Injury Act that protects a citizen's right to sue pharma companies when the company had the technological ability to make a vaccine less toxic but refused to do it. We want to bring to notice of*

> *Public Court of Industrial Malpractice that a few activist judges lobbying for Medici are attempting to rip the liability safety net from the mass vaccination system and virtually try to write Big Pharma a blank cheque by deliberately ignoring the language and legislative history of the old Vaccine Injury Act. This is not public health. This is exploitation of captive people by a pharmaceutical industry seeking unlimited profits and by doctors in positions of authority, who have never seen a vaccine they did not want to mandate. It is a drug company stockholder's dream, a healthcare consumer's worst nightmare and a prescription for tyranny. Any consideration of Medici's plea will give many drug companies total liability protection against injuries and deaths caused by state-mandated vaccines, and that will betraying the public.'*

Medici had turned a deaf ear to Molly Limaye's requests for Heal pill trial results. Not only had they stonewalled her queries with the standard 'drug trials results are the property of the drug companies that have paid for them' reply, but the company's PR firm was mailing her glowing reviews and favourable reports published in respected medical journals.

Molly had drawn a blank in tracing the authors of those reviews, and increasingly suspected the articles were being floated by the PR firm to form the circle of evidence that the company was using to drive sales. One adverse report could lead to demands to re-design the drug. Years of delay and billions spent on research could go down the drain...reputation of the company put on the line. What lengths a company would go to keep all that from getting away? Molly has a sneaking suspicion she may find out soon enough.

20

Binky Mendez
Friday, 13 November
Apartment No. 52, Verona (Building facing Molly Limaye's apartment)

The rented apartment in Verona is dark and gloomy. It is also stone cold and opens on three sides to a drainage. But Binky Mendez has paid twice the market rate to get this flat. The reason lies in the location of the flat's kitchen window. It gives a bird's eye view of the entire front ramp leading to apartment no. 503 on the fifth floor of the adjacent Glengate building. It is the ninth day of Binky Mendez's noiseless surveillance of Molly Limaye's apartment. He pats himself on the back for not just being circumspect enough to get the girl tailed—and also for being smart enough to rent the apartment which had a direct view at the entry to Molly's apartment. The telling bunch of high definition telephoto lens pictures taken during the surveillance of the journalist had proved that Binky's suspicions were not unfounded. He has just settled down with his camera when he sees something which sets his heart racing. Not only is a strange man snooping around the journalist's apartment but he has just dropped a packet at her place which is strange because he does not wait to get a delivery slip signed by her and disappears into the street. Binky's mind is in a whirl. The way the man was dressed it was impossible to guess his age or identity. But there was something about the man's body language which set Binky's stomach aflutter. Binky is still deciding on whether he should try to get his hands on the packet when the telephoto lens zooms onto someone so totally unexpected that it makes his eyes bulge with shock.

Kimmy White and Ranganathan, the Medici lawyer, are walking into the Yellow Bar and Lounge together!

Binky is utterly baffled but that does not derail his thinking process. He is not a man of just lucky hunches but is also known for his quick decisions. With lightning speed he removes his thick windbreaker, muffler and cap, and dons a burqa which he keeps handy for a range of surveillance activities to get his answers including for snooping on people or for quick getaways and such. Binky has decided the journalist puzzle will have to wait. His priority now is to find out what the hell Kimmy White is upto!

21

Ranganathan
Friday, 13 November
Yellow Bar and Lounge

'Did anyone see you?' Ranganathan asks Kimmy.

'I think I was exceedingly careful. I don't know if I should be here,' Kimmy said softly.

'Listen. You don't think you are doing us a favour, do you? You are here because your lover is a cheating bastard.'

Kimmy's composure lay in heap at his words. 'I don't expect him to be the Pope. He is a superstar.'

'So, you would rather indulge in a dreamy confusion about his motivations?'

'Just because I am not frothing at the mouth—'

'Hey shusshh, missy!' Ranganathan holds up an ominous finger, 'because the fact is you are raging mad that another woman, and technically your stepdaughter, has moved into your lover's bed. But enough of that. Have you got it? '

The colours on Kimmy's face mix up and the dim light brings out the swollen rims of her eyes in sharp focus, making them look like slivers of red meat.

'But we have watched your conduct. Despite a young head on your shoulder you have everything in you which makes you a suitable candidate as the next brand ambassador of Medici. Once that happens you will leave the Rathi Thackrays far behind…' At this point, Kimmy's girdle face briefly cracks and a slight furtive smile plays around the corner of her lips and she says, 'Rathi Thackray is neither pretty, nor talented. Unless one has a taste for the crass—'

'Good. Now shall we go through the stuff?'

Kimmy hands over the bag to Ranganathan and sits back.

'Wow.' Ranganathan whistles, finally impressed—this time the smile is genuine.

'I got something else too…' With a triumphant smile she reaches into her massive handbag and retrieved a small laptop into which she plugs in a data-card. Ranganathan watches with growing wonder.

Both of them fail to notice the burqa-clad woman eavesdropping on their conversation.

Half an hour later, Kimmy and Ranganathan leave and go on their individual ways. The woman in burqa too leaves the restaurant and gets into a waiting car. Inside the garment Binky Mendez's heart pounds with fury at Kimmy White's betrayal.

1993

It was with great difficulty that I gathered the courage to look at Buddhi. Or what remained of her. Her hands ended in rusty stubs from where the fingers had been chopped off. Not a stitch of cloth on her body, if I could still call it a body, with bruises and burn marks. Two pathetic black holes remained where her eyes had been gouged out. The slippery feel of the tissue, the flesh turning fluid, the smell of death made me nauseous and I vomitted. This was the punishment meted out to Buddhi by the same people she had tended to in their sickness for years. Buddhi's fate had been sealed with the rumour that the medicine prepared by her was responsible for the sudden death of two pregnant women and the birth of three blind newborn babies. When some children disappeared people blamed black magic and witches and human sacrifice. The headman and a few factory men, including Mr Sonny, held a village meeting where they got Hiri to swear that Buddhi practiced witchcraft and had sacrificed the children to increase her strength. That was all they needed. Hiri's lies had damned Buddhi but I could not believe Hiri had betrayed us. That night I went to Hiri's house to question her but she was not there. I found her at the factory. She was wearing a simple white dress, her shapely calves shone like upside down rolling pins in the dark. She was with the actor, the one whose face adorned the walls of the movie hall. I watched her suck her lover's body. And then there was another man who touched Hiri in a way which made me burn. I knew even then that both had

had her. It was too late to get her back.

That night when the villagers, led by the headman, Mr Sonny and some factory men barged into our house they locked mother and me in a room and dragged Buddhi away. I heard from others that her torture had been long and drawn out. They had gouged out her eyes and used hammers to extract her teeth and hung her from an old banyan tree. Mother cut the body down the following morning, but a mob soon formed demanding that it be hung again. She refused and the mob began hitting her, snatching the body away, they dragged her too and warned me they would come back for me next. I searched for Mother all day and finally found her lying senseless and soaking wet in the middle of the street near our house, her eyes unreadable, her face the colour of autumn. Mother warned me to hide in the Dune forests and I did not know that the next time I would see her would be when she was being murdered. And then never again. Anger raged inside me as I gathered Buddhi's broken bones and torn limbs into a stiff mound. Ignoring her hair that was enmeshed in my foot, I hugged the stony walls of the pit covered with slivers of her flesh and rubbery blood and took my first step towards light in days. Slowly, I inched my way out.

It was cold and raining when I walked back to the village.

22

Hiri
Saturday, 14 November
The Dune

Hiri does not want to sleep. She does not want to be awake either. The ghost finds her both ways. She moves in the affectless manner of the emotionally terrorized in whom fear and guilt has sunk its claws deep. She is scared the ghost will be back. His gaze troubles her, unlocks a mad wind in her head. She better not sleep she tells herself but her tired eyes close with fatigue and she descends into a nightmare. The ghost is ready on the bed for her. Hiri takes his name again and again as she waits for him to plunge deep inside her. But then the ghost's face changes, and keeps changing. She wants to wake up but he is too strong. A sad-faced child crawls out of her like red foam over a vat's black dripping sloping sides and it fills her with a mad desire to die. When she wakes up the ghost is standing right next to her bed.

'Get out!' She hides her face under the pillow.

The ghost bends down and kisses Hiri's icy lips. She tries to scream, to call out for her daughter but no word escapes her mouth.

'Hiri, its me. You know me, don't you? You, Buddhi, and me… in the mountains?'

It could be the softness in his voice or his words or the way light falls on his face that in an unexplained moment of lucidity she recognizes him. With recognition comes terror.

'You... it can't be you... How can it be you?'

'Hiri...'

'Why are you here?'

'I have come for you, Hiri...'

'Get out! You are a ghost—you cannot be alive!'

'Ghost? I am as much a ghost as you are Hiri. As we all are.' He says with infinite gentleness.

'Get away from me!' Hiri's voice is weak. She knows there is no point running from ghosts anymore. Two red sparks flash in the sodden darkness of the man's eyes. She suddenly wants him to be merciful. And when he touches her face gently she wants him to love her again.

'What happened to you, Hiri? Why did you let it happen?'

'He... he told me to... he said he will take me with him—he said he will love me if I said... if I said that she did it... that's all I did... that's all... I did... what did I do...' and the room is filled with her deranged wails.

Hiri feels his hands against her throat, hands which could have strangled her in an instant but do not yet. He holds her and caresses her and kisses her and she is crying and he tells her he is there to make the constant screams inside her head stop and to make her spirit go to the happy place and she relaxes and smiles a beautiful smile.

The man watches Hiri's mouth go slack, her eyes become whiter than marble and her body droop till she lay like a pile of dirty clothes. When it is over he is drenched in sweat. Eyes streaming with tears he lifts Hiri's lifeless body. He presses his lips on her head one final time. The men responsible for his pain would pay dearly.

23

Aslam Kapadia
Saturday, 14 November
Medici Studio

> Third and final notice to Mr A. Kapadia to share the script for final scene of *Healers*. The repercussions of your not doing so will not just be financial.
>
> —Rani Nadda, Chief Creative Consultant, Medici.

If Aslam hated anything more than being ordered around—it was women ordering him around. The genesis point of his hatred for women can perhaps be traced back to a humiliating incident from his childhood. He had been caught masturbating by his cousin and she had told her friends who had teased him mercilessly for months, *'Pervert, wanker, freak!'* He never forgot their mocking laughter at his humiliation of being made to feel smaller than his cock.

In such a state of lopsided emotional demographics, Aslam collects Medici's new creative consultant Rani Nadda's latest memo. And like any bully with an unrelenting misogynist streak he wants a scapegoat to vent his anger on. That scapegoat is to be Kimmy White the sole woman on the set.

'The scene where Kimmy White gets raped, just grab, punch and kick her at the same time. Use knives, sticks, ropes, the works—let it be a gang rape scene—many men coming at her like a pack of wolves. This is going to be the best rape scene ever—she needs to be beat up bad. Bleeding, muscle destruction—just brutal. A broken jaw maybe, at the very least she should certainly lose some teeth…'

'Mr Aslam, I have certain objections…' Kimmy says in panic.

'Sure. Stick a fork in yourself and open yourself up. Reveal your pearls to the world, bimbo.'

'You cannot talk to me like that! This scene is gross!'

'The gang rape or the underwater swim with the dead dog. Choose.'

'But I don't want to go underwater with a dead dog…! Get me an artificial one. '

'Kimmy White, why would we spend money on an expensive toy when we have dead dogs and cheap whores available for free?' Aslam smirks. 'And…it's not like I am using bolt-cutters to cut off your toes—though the audience cheers every time that happens too—one would think it would be easier than the blowjobs your character majors in—'

'Stop this. We can't allow women to be talked to like that, Mr Aslam!' The thin, high-pitched voice belonged to Rani Nadda. A thin-chested woman with sharp eyes which were slanted near both the eye's corners like beakers with a mouth on both ends, the shape of her face an almost perfect cone. She is the new Chief Creative Consultant for *Healers*. When Rani Nadda speaks she reveals a mouthful of teeth which gives Aslam the feeling of looking into the mouth of a serrated bear-trap.

'Would be good for you to understand that *Healers* is Medici's gift to public,' the woman said blowing huge smoke rings into the air. She is not really batting for Kimmy, but Rani Nadda would like people to know that she wilfully stood up for women's rights.

'Ideally, this film scene should have no breast shots and less blood.'

'The scene actually has one-third of breasts, and two-third of blood.' Aslam is sarcastic but his mid-section tenses so tight bullets could bounce off it.

'Wowiee! That's so cool that you can get it down that exact and all,' Rani retorts. 'So, do the actors and actresses vie for the boob time?'

'Uh, well we talk to all of them ahead of time so that they know exactly how much of the breasts are on show. It's a creative process.' Aslam is not willing to give up.

'Creative, my ass! Medici will not let women be treated like scum in *Healers*. I will need to look at the script. I am sure the late Mr Thackray discussed his ideas with you.'

No. He didn't, you witch! The paranoid son of a bitch... that so-called legend never showed me anything. I have no script! Nothing!

'I have incorporated an idea from Korean video game—it's kind of cool—'

'Why does the hero have to have a scar on his face?' Rani Nadda butts in.

'Its a parting gift from the man who raped his sister?' Aslam replies.

'Why does the hero have a scene on a Pierre Arnaud motorbike? It's expensive!'

'Why? Because I want it like that,' Aslam said tightly.

'No. It's not about what you want. It's about what the audience wants. Glorious fight sequences, macho fantasies of revenge is all fine but we need to yank it all back and stab them through the eyeball. This shit is too predictable.'

'I suppose a stoned hero wearing a pink shirt and firing from one building into the window of another to shoot the villain is predictable too?' He retorts.

'The hero is Medici's property—we cannot show him in an

embarrassing way. The script, Aslam—NOW!'

'Cannot. It's azaan time.' Aslam's jaw locks and he turns beet red. His anger is right out in the open now, bright and pulsing like a boil.

'You can't be serious! Isn't that supposed to be only on Friday?'

'No. That's Jumah. I do that too.'

'I want to see the script for God's sake, man.'

'You shouldn't take God's name in vain.'

In the commotion, no one notices Stud striding upto the elevated stage with his left arm curled against this midriff. He is holding small-sized rocks he has picked up from the edge of the sets. He selects a stone the size of a tennis ball and draws his hand back to his ear and throws the stone with full might. The stone whizzes past Aslam's left temple and falls harmlessly on the road.

'Aye! Stop it—whoever it is—you are dead!'

The second rock, a potential tooth smasher, passes two inches over Rani Nadda's head. Aslam almost wishes the stone cracks open her feminist skull. She would hang him out to dry if she knew he had no script in place. He imagines Thackray grinning at him with his maggot-infested skull.

Unless.

The clouds in the sky gathered and the horizon seemed to open up with blazing peals of electricity ripping it apart. A sign from Allah, he thinks feeling his habitual quickness return. Aslam retrieves a gossamer blue jacket which contains Thackray's incomplete script of *Healers*. He carefully attached his rejected storyboard sketches, which Thackray had once thrown into the dustbin. No one would come to know. If it worked he would take the credit, if it didn't they would be writing the fucking legend's obituary. Aslam laughs again for a full minute before he realizes that he hasn't smiled in weeks.

24

Dorab Silva
Saturday, 14 November
Police Canteen, South City Police HQ
Case no. 55/63/2018/dineshthackray/

The officers' mess smells of over-heated oil. The floor is a faded green linoleum—a rolling topography of hills and valleys, the woodwork greasy and dark. Three massive ceiling fans paddle away the heated air. The fat-soaked servings can make you a candidate for chronic cholesterol. Yet it was always hard to find a table at Bau's joint. Standing on a small square of the linoleum holding a done to death dish towel was Chef Bau, looking the same as he did twenty years ago, yellowish with a splotchy apron full of stains of coffee, curry, mutton, grease, chicken blood and God knows what else.

'Do you want see the breakfast menu or do you remember it?' Bau enquires in a thick accent from behind the counter with a geniality which comes with long association.

'Do you still make the Deluxe Bombay Steak Burger?' Gouda asks without looking at the grease-stained menu. Bau nods with a salute and Silva is relieved that unlike his untidy apron, the cook's nails are clean.

'When did she call, boss?'

'Last night, she said her mother was dead. A heart attack.'

Este had been crying when she called him and Silva doesn't feel the need to tell Gouda that he had promised to visit her. He feels strange his thoughts are with Este rather than the cracked husk of her mother who died inhabiting a world of shadowy memories.

'I am not surprised at all. Did you see her that day, boss? Crack-brained enough and already halfway to China. Must have been toking on dank nugs and spouted her innards into some pipe. Cooky as a broken whistle—you know if I ever had to do her mortem I would look inside her head, and not her viscera.' Gouda signals at Bau to hurry with the order.

'You know what they say about madness,' Silva said, 'that you can't go back to normal.'

'Well, at least, that explains the Valentine poster!' Gouda smirks and adds, 'Maybe the old coot was creaming on Mr Hero?'

'But is that all? There is something off. A famous director and a superstar are secret members of an underground club of pill poppers known for its fetish sex—FetLife. And Mina Meh sweared Hiri was an honorary member of the cooky club. Might have known a few secrets?'

'And now, the director is dead. And this woman is dead too—', Gouda's words are snuffed out by the sound of the tallow as it flops on the steaming pan.

'Remember the marks on her body—dermal defacing neo-thaumeturgist sort of thing. A very expensive hobby, I checked on Google. Who was paying for her pleasure?' Silva wonders aloud. Gouda takes a huge bite off the Deluxe Bombay Steak Burger and concentrates on devouring a major chunk of it before he replies.

'Exactly, boss. And by the looks of it she must have mainlined half her life. Fucking time bomb. Maybe meth mixed with X—some of that crap hits high—very expensive too. So, the question remains. How the fuck did she get the drugs?'

'Boss...boss, are you okay? Hey, boss!' Gouda asks worriedly. *So, how did she get it?*

A walking time bomb—you should have known—did you know it was a girl?

There was a baby girl in his wife's stomach. He did not know that she was pregnant when he offered to drop his wife to the hospital after a night of experimenting with meth balls. Nobody had expected the big van would back up and swerve in the middle of the road.

'I am fine. Just forgot the goddamn pills.'

The men pause and stare at each other saying nothing.

'Its okay, boss.'

'Listen, I have to visit Este… I mean Hiri's daughter, it will take some time. Don't wait up for me. Is my car at the grade crossing?'

'Yes, boss. But will you drive?'

'Fuck off.'

'Okay, boss. And I will file the report and send you a copy. Have to check with the forensics—the drill—hope we have some answers soon.'

'It's not about finding answers. It's about managing expectations.' It was Silva's dead wife's favourite saying. She had been trying to say that the day she died.

The memory cloudburst swallowed him whole and he remembered the mini-van pull out in front of him, but it was too late. The colour of the van changed every time he thought of the accident as if the camera in his head was adjusting the saturation point till the image was drained of all colour. His wife was thrown against the wheel which carved a blunt arc on her chest. The next moment she was not on her seat and when he stumbled out of the car he saw her lying in a parking lot with her purse still over her shoulder and an uneaten chocolate in the hand. It had been a baby girl.

Silva extracts a dark medicine case and gobbles two pints of the colourless tincture straight from the prescription glass bottle, for today and yesterday, and painful tomorrows.

25

Saturday, 14 November
Este and Silva
Case no. 55/63/2018/dineshthackray/

Este's flat, the Dune

That Este has left the door open Silva thinks to be a fortuitous omission on her part. Her room is very small, a bunk bed, a cabinet, a small TV, a tiny fridge, two chairs and a small writing table make for her furniture. But there is a certain beauty in arrangement of things or perhaps it is the effect of the apricot-coloured light of the summer streaming through the small panels of the window. By the windowsill is her picture holding her baby, framed in a row of seashells. She is beautiful in her own way, he recalls his wife's favourite quote by Carletti—'Beauty is a summation of parts working in such a way that nothing needs to be added, taken away or altered.' Silva finds it ironic that a whore has brought out the poet in him. Born to a woman like Hiri, Este would have known pretty early about her limited options. She looks like an ordinary girl, a beautiful girl, and it bothers him that she looks so completely accepting of a life so damned. When she comes to meet him she is wearing only a slip and there is a way about her that causes the dull ache in his chest to build with unexpected intensity. And then it happens. Like it has been sitting, crouching, inside his body—a starved beast. Before he knows it, he is fucking her. As he gets into her she drops onto her back getting rid of her wet clinging underpants and tosses them on top of his clothes on the floor. His fingers spread in the hollow of her back crushing her soft arms, her chest. The intensity of his release brings him down to his knees and she is on her stomach and he takes her again. He has a happy tiredness, which comes after making love in the deepest of ways, the way it was with his wife. He can always blame it on her perfume or not having felt a woman's touch in five years. But who was asking? Este suddenly reaches out and touches his face. 'Who are you mourning? Who was she?' she asks.

A stunned Silva goes quiet for a moment. And then he hears himself talk to Este.

'My wife.'

'Men look for mothers in their wives I have heard. Do I look like her?' Este asks.

'You two couldn't be more different.' He is not completely honest and a part of him wonders that he is sharing his most intimate details with a prostitute he has met on a street while working on a murder case. Sensing his bewilderment, Este moves away from him.

'Who found her body?' he asks her and wonders why he isn't being able to ask her the right questions. This was supposed to be investigation after all.

'I did. I did not realize she was dead till it was already high noon.'

'I am sorry.'

'Don't be. The spirit had abandoned her long ago. I didn't recognize her in what was left. The stench was terrible—she had been unwell for long, you saw yourself how she was in the end. Didn't even recognize me...in the end I think I was almost a stranger to her.'

In the night's glow, Este's body seemed to be wrapped in shadows like that of moth-wings and a sudden intense emotion grips him and he wants to breathe her in—her wet hair and freshly cleaned body and that milky smell. Silva finds her more and more irresistable. He sucks at her nipples. They taste warm and smooth and a little like peaches. He puts his arm around her waist and feels the smooth texture of her skin. When he kisses her, she kisses him back with equal passion.

'You are old enough to be my daughter,' he reflects.

'But I am not your daughter,' she says, and he enters her with a desperation which stuns him. A photo frame falls from a shelf and they laugh at the unexpected noise it makes. Later on while smoking a cigarette, he looks at the same photo. It's not a very old picture and he can make out Este, looking happy and standing close to a man who is holding her baby. A family photo that had the air of peace and security. The man has very prominent cheekbones and sharp looking eyes, making him look like a professor. He stares at the photo intently.

'Is something the matter?' Este asks.

'Just my overworked brain making connections—is he the baby's father?' he asks while trying to hide his embarassment.

'Damn no! No fathers, no daughters here.'

Silva realizes there were certain questions which should not be asked of a whore.

'He is an uncle. He helps us out sometimes,' Este said with a faraway look and Silva wonders why he is so ready to believe her. A part of him knows why. The girl starts a slow movement with her torso, which is more sensuous than anything he had ever seen. She looks like the culmination of all the sex goddesses, he has ever fantasized about. She was what he had missed in the last five years. If she touched him now he knew he would come at once. The lust he feels for her is unbearable.

'Touch me,' he hisses hotly into her ears and she laughs.

'Hold still or—' the world around him explodes in an orgasm so deep and strong that he thinks it would simply tear him apart. He sinks next to her, feeling powerless.

'I told you I was fun.'

'I knew you would be fun.'

He starts feeling drowsy. That is when he notices a Valentine poster flashing a knowing grin. He notices the actor's face in the poster has been damaged like someone in great rage has attacked it. May be it is time to pay the Superstar a visit.

26

Neville Valentine
Saturday, 14 November
Medici Studio
Shooting of Healers in progress

The six spikes of the burnished metal hexagram sparkle in the blaze of the studio lights. It is a burnt gold hexad, a well accepted symbol of spiritual healing. It is the backdrop of the lavish set created for a special scene of *Healers*: An exclusive stunt to be filmed on Valentine which involves an enormous Daniel Chopper superbike. The bike itself is a monstrous metallic contraption specially commissioned by Pierre Arnaud, Medici's newly appointed film stylist for the project. It's a long and tiresome process. The giant superbike is slowly raised with aerial suspension hoists clasped to the ceilings and monstrous hooks. Finally in place, it sits in the air like a savage abnormality.

'Ya Allah!' mutters Aslam.

'What a place to find Allah in. Am I to ride that demon?' Valentine is awestruck.

'*Mon Dieu*! Isn't she a Goddess. *Un belle desse*…a beautiful Goddess for our screen God!' Pierre tells Valentine.

'Can we ride your Goddess?' Aslam scoffs as if a constantly undervaluationary response is the only thing he is capable of.

'*Non…non*! Not ride, Monsieur Aslam Kapadia! *We don't ride the Goddess!* We RISE with the Goddess!' Pierre retorts.

'Sure. No big deal.'

'NO BIG DEAL? *Qu'est que c'est*! It's a bigger deal than any deal! I give you the colossus…a metal Goddess who will strike fear into heart of villans and you say "No Big Deal"! *Mon travail est le meilleur oui*…my work is the best Mr Aslam Kapadia!'

A 500cc engine, scintillating double-sided swing arm, mirror classic chrome, and 300mm rear tire awaits Valentine.

'This is easy. I can do this with my eyes closed,' Valentine says with a confidence that doesn't quite reach his eyes. The bike is raised to a point where it stands precariously suspended, a good 50 feet away from the ground. It takes a full hour before Valentine is hoisted on the superbike secured by a braided cable, his feet anchored in sturdy restraints. A thick cluster of belts, straps and tackles held the monstrous superbike in space. In order to create a dynamic physical tension between metal and flesh, Boy's genius has endowed the star with extra irridescence. Valentine's lean and taut physique looks stunning juxtaposed against the monster bike. Everyone gasps when the machine starts shaking as if gripped in the throes of a mid-air super torque—and Valentine looks like a demigod with a magnificently muscled body.

In the beginning, the commotion below does not draw his attention but when Aslam and others stare at him and back at the computer, Valentine feels the first prick of uneasiness. The fifteen minutes it takes for Valentine to be unharnessed and get to the ground seem like forever. He pushes through the men who are riveted by what looks like a crudely shot and badly edited video of a man and a woman in a bathtub giggling and snorting; the camera moves closer to the shot of his tongue on Rathi's breast. Thick shock sinks in Valentine.

'It's on the Internet. Someone has posted this on the Internet!

It is getting record views.' Aslam keeps on repeating like a madman. And ordinarily a mix of manic creativity and instant suggestions, this time even Pierre is stumped.

'Bad for art! *Les femmes stupides sont mauvais pour l'art*! Never mix women and art.'

A soft growl works up from somewhere inside Valentine and lodges in his larynx not letting air in or out. He almost doesn't hear the set assistant's nervous rush of words.

'Mr Valentine, ACP Dorab Silva is on his way to meet you regarding the Dinesh Thackray case, Mr Ranganathan is on the phone for you regarding some "moral clause violation". And Mr Binky Mendez is demanding to speak to you—he has something very important to tell you about—about the viral video…'

The next few minutes that Valentine is on the phone with Binky see him riveted to the phone. He rushes towards the east wing of the Medici Studio which houses the junior stars, straight to Kimmy White's room.

༚

Kimmy handles the disastrous turn of events rather well. All she asks for is to be allowed to collect her personal belongings. There was no denying the fact that Kimmy's world had come crashing down. She is baffled as to how Binky Mendez got to know about her secret meeting with the lawyer. She leaves the sets without a word of protest and revenge in her heart.

Build your hatred. Take revenge on those who trespass against you.

The neo-thaumeturgists' code proposed an unconventional interpretation of vengeance. Taking revenge on Binky will be the best part, she promises herself.

27

Silva and Valentine
Saturday, 14 November
Valentine's Chamber, Medici Studio
Case no. 55/63/2018/dineshthackray/

'Desolate, isn't it? No pictures on the walls, no awards, medals. Unusual for a superstar you may be thinking?' Valentine's drawl breaks the oppressive silence in the chamber when he catches Silva staring at the room's minimalistic décor.

'Now that you mention…'

'I enjoy the feeling of space. Always disliked the emotional trappings of crippling family memories, flimsy relations or medals once acquired. Wasteful and ruinous. But I am about to make space for my new acquistion.' Valentine points towards the painting of a man standing on a high cliff staring transfixed at the cypresses of some anonymous garden in the backdrop of a distorted rainbow. The woeful figure conveyed the feeling of intense loneliness.

'It's by a young talented artist. A fan. He gave it to me for free. Stupid boy. He will never make it big. Probably will die penniless. You see talent is nothing if you cannot market and sell your product. As someone said we are all supplies,' Valentine says. 'One should make people pay your price.'

'Did Mr Thackray also pay the price?'

'Depends on what he was buying, I assume. But I have no

idea. Of course I do wonder what Thackray must have felt when his body ripped over a hundred metres with nothing but air to break his fall. Sorry if I come across as too cold. But if you assume this industry stops to mourn, sorry to disappoint you. We have pressures of the kind which make a normal man demented, sentiments are the first casualty.'

'Mr Thackray had pressures? Any you were aware of?'

'If he jumped out of a window he must have had. Or if he was pushed as the media is speculating—'

'Conjecture. Till we find the proof.'

'The media—there should be a law against them. Stabbing and jabbing with their beaky conjectures and premature opinions. Always so quick to pronounce judgement on our dimming beauties and hollow cheeks and thinning hair and dull eyes…self-appointed monitors of our waking hours,' Valentine slices a piece of passion fruit. The tarty citrus smell disperses in the still air. He takes a sliver while holding the steel knife like a butcher only to spit it out in disgust.

'Ppttthooo…this is rotten!'

'Tastes perfectly fine to me,' Silva munches on a small bite.

'Maybe mine was rotten. Sorry, I am not keeping well. I have brushed thrice since morning, using the mouthwash liberally but it's only gotten worse—but that's not what you came to hear, did you?'

'What can you tell us about Dinesh Thackray?'

'We were similar. We were different.'

'How would you describe your relationship with Mr Thackray?'

'Like two people wed for long—every comedy, every tragedy, every farce was played out. What was left was artificial and cruel. You know officer, the real tragedies in life happen in such inartistic manner, like death and love and parents. Crudely vulgar, entirely lacking of style and coherence.'

'Did he ever mention being scared of someone? Any secrets he shared?'

'We all have our own secrets. Don't you? Maybe he suffered as much. Who can tell now.'

'There are some pictures of him with a girl… Do you recognize her?' Silva pushes Hiri's picture in front of Valentine.

'No, who is she?'

'She lived at the Dune.'

A silent look passes between the two men.

'From the Dune, is it? So, what you really want to know is if Thackray liked the company of whores. So what if he did? Don't you?'

'You have not answered the question.'

'Women shan't be understood and whores will remain undiscussed. Perhaps I am not the person you should be talking to about Dinesh's maladies. But this picture… may I ask you how you came upon it?'

'Pictures of this girl were found hidden in Thackray's house. We don't know yet whether she is related to his death.'

Valentine looks at the picture in his hand as if amazed that such a thing had found its way into his hand. Silva notices the star's gaze is skewed as if he is avoiding looking at the girl's face by fixing his gaze at some point behind her.

'Why not ask the girl?' Valentine asks.

'She is dead. Did you by any chance know her?'

'No.'

'She had your posters in her room.'

'Officer! That's not a crime. Yet.' Valentine laughs a glorious laugh.

'No, it is not. But she did this to your poster before she died,' Silva shows him the poster.

'An angry fan? Did not like my movies? An extreme reaction… but you can never tell with fans,' Valentine glanced at his watch and got up, an indication that the meeting is over.

'Sorry, but I have no clever lines for you. I am afraid that perhaps its true what my detractors say, that without the parts to act and without the lines to say what would I be? Just a man with not two lines to call my own! Please excuse me—my make-up has cracked—come, Boy, you have come just in time. The police officer was just leaving.'

Silva finds flat and depthless eyes staring at him nervously and he shakes his head.

'I believe in cooperating with the law even if I still don't know what you could possibly want from me—are you fine? You are sweating, Officer!'

※

The moment Silva leaves, Valentine slumps on the couch, completely exhausted. Shivers run down his spine and an unreasonable fear chokes him. Holding the warm cigarette smoke inside his chest doesn't help and the sweat on his chest slowly congeals into ice. The micro-dosing punches him in the eye and he feels trapped in a weird head space with fucked tolerance and still miles from levelling out. He should have let his serotonin levels balance out before prepping. But it is cheap price for some sleep—even if a chemical sleep without dreams, without real rest.

When Ranganathan walks in unannounced, Valentine eyes him dully.

'Get out,' Valentine's voice is hoarse.

'Really? No thanks, I will stay. This is Medici property. Should I make you a drink?' Ranganathan's lips hang like a mulish child and there is a sullen silence of censorship about him.

'I heard you had visitors?'

'Yes. The police were here.'

'The police, huh? This is getting too troublesome. We had a moral clause, may I remind you—

'What I should care about is your taint rubbing off my shine. Your *flawed* business could make me appear a criminal too, don't you think?' Valentine said tiredly pressing his head, 'besides, the day people value morality you too will have to shut shop. If I were you I would wish for people scurrying about in sick perversions'. The two men eye each other like old predators well-versed with the each other's hunting patterns.

'What did they want?'

'The police came to show me a photo of a prostitute—aaahh, Boy!' Valentine screams at Boy when his hand slips and turns a muscle in the wrong direction.

'Are you trying to skin me?' Valentine angrily pushes away Boy's palm.

'I'm sorry, mister! Extremely sorry. My hand slipped on the latex—'

'Is this real gold?' Ranganathan stares at the shimmering golden latex cream on Valentine's arms and legs.

'Yes, sir,' Boy replies with pride, 'this liquid latex colour I have created, it meshes with flesh tones well. I can create dimensional textures with beads or sand like the one in your last scene—'

'Boy, STOP! Binky is right! You take your craft too seriously—go both of you leave me alone!'

'There should be no hard feelings—'

'You fucking pervert, you have too big a view of your importance—your bloody company owes me! You talk about morality with your damned little whore boys! The ones you hide in your house for your pervert acts. What? The poor boys you keep occupied during the day so you can sink your testicles into them at night, you asshole!' Ranganathan opens his mouth and closes it, like a fish gasping for air. He leaves without a word.

'Boy, please don't put that cream on me again. It makes me short of breath.'

'Sir, this is a different cream—a much better one. It is much easier to remove and no obnoxious fumes. You will not feel sick anymore.' With a strong hand, Boy scoops out a lotion and mixes some body balm into it and applies it on the traces of paint on Valentine's neck and shoulders till the Superstar shines with a kinglike beauty. But Valentine isn't feeling any different from a naive artist who uses bitumen as a varnish to produce startling brilliance unaware that the germ of radioactivity has already polluted the solvent, leading to a destructive chemical reaction.

28

Rathi Thackray
Saturday, 14 November
The Dune

Rathi Thackray had driven for more than half a day in the Dune settlement and her fingers were sticky and swollen from the briny air. The unnaturally bright sun made it difficult to drive, made worse by tenements crowded close together and separated by narrow lanes with dusty untarred roads and Rathi had to stop several times for directions to 'Roobi Bloo'.

It is now almost dusk and Rathi is feeling increasingly disoriented in the sea of zinc roofs which shine like dirty puddles and the air stinky with the smell of shit and she is scared at the thought of being trapped in a place like this by the approaching darkness. Not only is she confused with respect to her exact geographical position but is unable to re-acquire a sense of orientation or summon up even a measure of confidence she felt at the start of her mission to go to Roobi Bloo. Not wanting to spend the night in the twisted maze of the old township she concludes that heading back would be a prudent choice. But going back the way she had come would mean several more hours at the Dune. Rathi finally decides to take a shortcut through the fish market, and through the tiny lanes bloated with meat shops, cassette retals, hairstylists and past naked toddlers with only strings of beads attatched to their fat tummies and young whores with sly looks. Time and again boys wearing caps working with fresh batches of fish block her path with their load of live and stinking sea creatures. By the time she crosses the fish market the wind has completely changed direction sending damp gusts of air. In the galloping darkness, there is a crackling crash of lightening. It throws a lance over the sky and illuminates a signboard ahead of her. Looking at it, Rathi feels part of some suspended reality. The paint on the board is swollen and the hues are mixed up so you cannot tell the rust from the rot but she can make out the words:

Welcome to Roobi Bloo

Instead of feeling jubilant, a sick feeling coats her stomach and she braces to run at the first sign of danger. From a distance, it looked nothing like the opium den of her nightmares where one can buy oblivion and more. A smattering of drunk and doped people, their faces and gait marked by substances, reel in and out through the swinging doors cursing anyone and everyone who cross their path and Rathi is grateful for the hard object in her purse and clings to it tenaciously as if gripping onto the last bit of security.

Approaching the tavern-shaped entry of Roobi Bloo, Rathi feels oddly in-sync with the jarring look of the place as if strangeness is now her one lasting reality. During the day it probably resembles a well-worn drinkery-saloon cum grog shop but as the night appraches Roobi Bloo becomes a sly whore ready to strike a killer deal. Not wanting to attract unwanted attention, Rathi takes refuge in the dimmest corner which also happens to be closest to the exit door. Leaning against the cheap leather seat she lights a reefer. It is stoked to a concentration she can handle and she waits for the sharp bite of the restorative fix to hit her. A couple of raucous girls and boys with crazily glazed eyes grab seats near her and order their drinks in shrieky voices. The tall, dark-skinned woman with long curly hair seems to be the leader of the group. 'Lil Lillette', her name, is spelled out in shiny gold alphabets on a thick chain around her neck.

'What's that you are creaming your face with, bitch? Diaper gravy?' Lil Lillette screams in disgust at another.

'Smells like dog shit. Get away from me, punk,' Lil Lilette yells at a small-faced boy.

'Runt faced faggot trash—back off.' Lil Lillette raises a fist at his gutted face.

'Slut, let me educate you this shit on my face is crud-mask, weed from the black sea—I eat it too—' the thin girl says.

'Putting putrefied dead flesh on your face so you can shake your fanny?' Lil Lillette yells and everyone laughs in chorus including the thin girl and the buck-toothed boy.

'Hey, little girl, wanna 4x4 V8 dick for dinner?' A group of drugged men hold out their hand towards Rathi and she shrinks back.

'Get lost, faggot. She don't want any you got—' Lillette shouts.

'Ayuuuuh because some lesbo love here—I can take both man!'

'Dang dog, you have a back!' Lil Lillette spreads her long dark legs strapped by high-heeled sandals around the ankles and makes to grind her hips short frenzied jabs.

The boys whistle and cheer, Rathi is relieved they are not interested in her anymore.

'A big shout out to the dudes trying to get laid—keep working on that grind your time will come… Keep trying, keep trying!' The girls started cheering and dragged the men to the dance floor. All except Lil Lillete, who sat content swearing and drinking.

'You new here? Haven't seen you before or have I?' Lil Lillette asks without bothering to look at her.

'I—I'm looking for someone,' Rathi decides to stick to the truth.

'Aren't we all, honey… aren't we all!'

Lil Lillette offers some dried meat cake, which Rathi takes with a smile. She thinks the appearance of friendliness is worth a great deal if only to initiate some sort of reciprocal cooperation. Munching on the spicy rubbery meat, Rathi retrieves the photograph and puts it before Lilette. When she sees recognition in Lil Lillette's eyes her heart began beating faster.

'What's she to you?'

'I am looking for her.'

'Well, I can't help you, girl. No one can.'

'Look I can pay you well—' said Rathi.

'Missy, no money can get you to where she is—she is dead. Plonked off a few weeks ago.'

'Dead?'

'Yup. But her daughter's there—name is Este—if you want any business with her,' she winks.

'Her daughter?'

'Yup. That's her… over there!'

In her excitement Rathi ignores the first symptoms. The sense of something off, the clammy sweat, the pinch in the left side of her rib cage. Lil Lillette points at a girl swaying in the dance floor to loud music. She cannot see her face clearly and she makes her way towards the dancing girl. But when the walls begin to close in she stops. A bitter iron taste coats her mouth and oozes down the back of her throat and she curses letting her guard down. Her fingers feel loose and Rathi drops her car keys, but doesn't hear the sound of it hitting the floor. The noise in the bar shreds her nerves and her head hurts but she is still on her feet and that is good. But she is too far from her car and that is bad. She curses herself for her stupidity.

What mad impulse had led her to this hellhole?

With an effort Rathi manages to put her mental blocks back in place and stumbles out of the bar. Enclosed in the locked safety of her car, she finally breathes a sigh of relief. It is short-lived when she sees people approach her and she checks the car's locks. The wind outside is howling and the road is thick with slurry. The car's engine takes time to shudder to life. Faces are peering inside the car and in a panicky confusion she slams on the accelerator which is a wrong move as the car goes ahead a few metres before it starts sinking into the rising slush. The cloudburst has turned the road into a mini river. The way the trees are swaying she knows she has to get out fast or be crushed like a bug in a glass cup. Dropping the gears into low range she moved a couple of notches into the emergency brakes and allows the engine to pull them. Something jams and the car's engine stops. The car is stuck in 10 feet of muddy water and inching dangerously towards a black brownish open gorge of gushing water. The car hits a bump and her head bangs on the metallic rim of the door several times with tremendous force. Forcing open the car door with a leg she tries to stand but her knees give out. Holding her head, she falls face down into the muddy water.

The first vision she has when she regains consciousness, is of her car rolling over and over as it goes down the current. The walls of the room she is in sway and she realizes she has not drowned. A quick look reveals no harm to her person. Her purse is lying neatly. And an unattended child is playing with her car keys. It's a sparsely furnished room with a square table covered by a small white oil cloth on one end and cheap jute stools and some plates, cups and saucers on the other. A hot gush of incredulity engulfs her but in her insensate state she fails to understand her own reaction. The air grows thin and she has trouble breathing when she tries to talk. The sound of sea drones in her ears. She is still at the Dune. The bruises on her head are on fire. The pain blowback will pass eventually she knows but she feels terribly weak.

'Her head looks bad…' she hears a voice say.

'You seem fine, missy. But you'll have one hell of a hangover!' The girl moves closer to her baby who is still engrossed with the car keys.

'What difference does it make? She is not going anywhere for quite sometime.' It takes her a minute to locate where the voice is coming from. The man is crouched at her feet. He is putting things back in her bag and she feels she has seen him before, only she cannot place where.

'Clummmmdyy—' her tongue is thick, rubbery.

'Where am I?' Rathi works her tongue around her mouth until she has enough saliva to moisten her throat.

'Now, miss! You are fine, now don't panic, you are fine. You are on medicine… no, don't move… you are too weak right now…'

Rathi starts to answer, but stops. In the room on a mantle-shelf was the photograph of the girl she has been looking for.

'Who… who's that? That girl… I am…. looking…. for her… Lillette says she is dead… dead?' holding her thrumming head she points at the photo.

'Yes. She is dead… but… you should try to sleep. The medicine won't work otherwise.'

'You… your face… you look like her! Who… are you? Where am I?'

The girl doesn't reply and continues to snuggle her child. Rathi's tongue feels limp as if with some potent drug. But she is not looking at the girl's picture anymore. The child playing with her car keys is chuckling at her delightfully. The pupil deformity is hard to miss. The abnormality has manifested itself even more strongly in the child's eyes. She wonders if the head injury she received has deliberately overlaid her dead father's face on every aspect of her memory section. One in ten million chance of anyone having it they had said. The rare gene which passed on for generations in her family—passed on from parents to children....from fathers to daughters. A window rattles in the rising wind and she wonders if that was the sound of truth storming in her head. She feels hot along the left side of her face...from behind her eye...through to the back of her head and sound, sight, scent are all crashing around her when she loses consciousness again.

Rathi wakes up in a large room, largely undecorated with pitted walls and basic woodwork. In her weakened state, she notices her car keys and bag with its contents are kept on a table.

'Don't be frightened—you are safe here.' Rathi hears the girl speak. She looks up at her face but her eyes are drawn to her baby who peeks from her breast, in a familiar sculptural symmetry.

'Who are you?' Rathi asks.

'I just told you...my name's Este. You are in my house.'

'Whose baby is that?' She has to know.

'Too many questions. But tell me from where did you get this picture of my mister and my mar'm?'

'What do you mean by "my mister"? Do you know that man?'

'Do I know him? Very well, I would say...but why should I tell you?'

'I am his daughter.'

'Mister's daughter! In my house too...fancy that.' Este's laughter offends Rathi. As much as what she said next.

'Fancy meeting Mister's other daughter!'

'Other?'

'You are looking at the other one, we are family, Missy!'

Rathi looks like she has been shot in the face.

'We are family. God's honour—if you believe in that sorta thing! See, Missy...you may have guessed my trade—at the Dune, not many options for hard-working girls. But the main thing is your father had occasion to be very close with me. He visited here often, it was all going well—he got me this room, gave me money, looked after me. What more does a whore want? And I finally got a patron—'

'Stop! Why are you telling me this?' Rathi wants to run but her legs don't budge.

'Have patience, Missy. So, when one day I am with this baby and—and I tell Mister, your father, the baby girl is his, and my mar'm laughs and laughs—she was a cold one...! And then she tells me the truth. Well, it turns out Mister knew Ma'rm too, not like you know people in your world but in the way we know men at the Dune—which is fine for lots of men here do ma'rms and daughters and some together—'

'Please Stop.' Rathi is ready to strangle Este to make her stop.

'Missy doesn't want to hear the truth? Don't you want to know what my ma'rm said?' Este lets the world drop on Rathi's head.

'Turns out, Mister is my pop too! Mar'm was mean and mocked him saying Mister now had two daughters in the Dune! Can you believe it? Mister said he had nothing to do with us—which is fine—for there are men who whore their own daughters and think nothing about it, he was not that kinda man. So you see Missy, we have the same pop...so, that makes us sisters. Three sisters! If you count little Kaayi!'

The little mite looks at Rathi with her innocent blue and gold speckled eyes. And Rathi feels damned for it.

29

Saturday, 14 November
Ranganathan's apartment

The man enters Ranganthan's apartment only after making sure that the lawyer has left the building. The little boy is crying soundlessly. He has been in pain all night. The infection is flaring up and the terrible pain has returned, he is sobbing in a tiny voice for help. The man gestures him to stay quiet and to calm down. He has gentle eyes and the boy instinctively relaxes. For the next half an hour the man applies ointment on the boy's affected part. He promises the little boy there would be no need for him to be scared of the bad man ever again. He looks at Ranganathan's photo and a fury rips through him. He has never hated a man more.

1993

I entered my house in the dead of the night. It had been broken into and looted several times. What marauders could not take they had trashed. The place smelled of urine and the walls were covered with graffiti and the smell of recent violence lingered. There was no sign of life. The rain and air had swollen the wooden wall and it was hard to peel it off to get to the hidden store room. Thankfully, it was intact. Forlorn but intact, having completely escaped the wrath of the intruders. Mother kept all her most treasured possessions in the secret storage room, including medicines, prescriptions and formulae and ingredients for important drugs. The chief storage area, almost a crawl space, had been floored with wooden pallets just to keep chemicals off the ground, was covered with dust. It had eroded in places to reveal the soil below and white fluid-like substance had leaked from the bottles and dried on the cracked cabinets which were lined with still more bottles and jars of yellow mushrooms, seeds, brittle flowers and herbs all soldered to their containers by the sticky dampness.

The cabinet marked with a circle in chalk was the one which harboured mother's most precious formulae. I dipped my hand inside it and my fingers closed on a dull white preserve box. Inside it was a green paste—gelatinous, opaque in lustre, waxy in texture, the odour persistent, heavy and cloying. These were the special medicines mother had been working on when they took her. Stuck to the back of the old cabinet were some papers soggy from mould and damp. The wood seemed hell-bent on clutching to the secrets but I shoved hard and managed to get the papers out in one piece. The papers were full of crucial notes on her work and exact empirical calculations of the new medicies she was preparing. There was a letter written by my mother to me, her final words. I read and re-read it many times till every word got ingrained in my head—

> *Am I a witch, Akhouri? The villagers tell me I am one. They destroyed all my medicines, everything they could get hold of when it could have been used to heal so many. If you find this letter it means the store room is intact… it has everything I value… The villagers say I used sorcery to kill their children. Company money has blinded them. They don't believe me that an invisible poison is settling in our soil and its coming from the factory waters. It is coming from the chemicals they are using in the factory. The rivers are suddenly full of the red fish… all the other fish—the pina, the yellow fish, the little fucus have all disappeared… all except the red lui. Workers from medicine factory told me secretly that compay is pumping the lui with silver to make it breed faster… which is poison for our people… you will not feel it now but over the years…*
>
> *But there is something worse I have to warn you about. I had gone to the factory to confront Mr Sonny and I saw him with our little children. Akhouri they saw me and will come to get me… you have to save our children, our girls—*

She was lost to me as a rainbow in a storm, as reason in madness. I could hardly breathe in my desire for revenge, I would make them pay for what they did I swore.

30

Ranganthan
Sunday, 15 November
Pied Piper Yatch, the Dune harbour

The *Pied Piper* has seen quite a bit of full blast partying. Once a month the luxury yacht, packed with top company executives, advertisers, celebrities and loaded to the gun-whales with liquor, would set sail from a private port. There are several intriguing tales about Medici's private boat of pleasure and Ranganathan knows them to be true as he steps into the *Pied Piper*. It's like entering an outlandish parallel universe programmed to persuade impulsive actions and reckless fantasies. A sensory overload of lasers and an intoxicant laden air which exudes a vulgar extravagance greets him, Ranganathan inhales deeply the smell of immense money and absolute power.

'Man, look at this scene!' says someone to someone and Ranga agrees.

'Wonky, wild, and demented. Just the way I love it.'

He stands overheated and overwhelmed, among the hordes of gawking viewers—all clamouring to get a look at the kinky displays, performers bound with rope to makeshift frames, some suspended in the air, others spanked, whipped and confined, bondage being the chosen theme of the day.

'Ah Ranga, there you are! Have you sampled some of our

delights yet?' a masked man hugs him and asks cheerily.

'Slowly honey, now I am an old man, not some drug raging beat your ass in the waffle house rock star! But what's life without a little adventure I say…' Feeling the rush of exciting possibilities Ranga's face split into a sly leer.

'Follow me—this way,' beckons the high spirited voice. Ranga hesitates for he is waiting for Kimmy. She had promised more 'explicit' evidence of Valentine blatantly flouting Medici's moral clause. But he allows himself to be dragged through the crowd like a wilful child.

'C'mon man! You are missing all the fun!' his masked companion grips his hand firmly and pushed through several thick curtains into a hall called the Pit. Ranga has heard about the Pit. The place has an air of stout impregnability. Girls in feathers and little else, looking like birds of heaven lead them to their secluded seats behind scented curtains. Mysterious vapours hover in the air and blend with the smell of smoke, sweat, and sex. Feeling a rush of adventure, Ranga settles on a silk sofa bed with its long backs stapled to the walls. Several things happen to him as he sits down and the significance of the tiny pinprick on his back goes unnoticed.

The Pit's spotlight was on a naked girl with vacant eyes gently swaying on a tiger-skin rug.

Her wrists and ankles tied with rope to a small metal bed frame, her body contorted at an awkward angle she writhes in ecstasy against her restraints. There is no attempt to stimulate any emotion for there is none. The overwhelmed audience holds their breath.

'That's something, eh?'

'More than a physical scratch for sure! But tell me do I know you, honey?' Ranga asks as he struggles to sit but his limbs strangely flap back into a limp position. He attributes it to the myriad opiates in the air. His companion has removed his mask and vague recognition dawns but for some inexplicable reason his mind is feeling unable to make the critical connection. As a result try as he might, Ranga is unable to place the man.

'I know you—maybe nog—not, whats happeninf—happening to me!' His words stick to each other as if glued together.

'And I know you, doctor. I know your secrets too.'

'Y—you—do?' Ranga begins to laugh uncontrollably and for no reason.

'That would be—something—is that frue—true—' Ranganathan repeats every word like a child wrapping his toungue about each syllable. Ranga increasingly finds that he is speaking with a heaviness similar to when a dentist shoots the mouth full of Novocain which slowly floods the lips, tongue and gums. But if that alarmed him, it was not to a degree to spur him into action yet.

In the second part of the show, the spotlight is on a mammoth fish aquarium bursting with several fishes. A giant ogre fish is slipped into the tank. The monster fish catches a dozen of the squirming fish in its jaws but within minutes a gulper eel unhinges itself from the dark and grabs the ogre fish with its enormous jaw. The audience watches in awe as the eel stretches its stomach to consume the massive ogre fish as big as itself, and drags it down into the dark waters.

'Sure is—something!' His words come out all mixed up.

'But not as much fun as the little boys?'

Ranga's eyes widen and he looks uncomfortable.

'Whatssdat—what's—that mean, honey?'

At that point Ranga's brain let his air-locked lungs kick in and he remembers where he has seen the man but its already too late. His limbs fail to move as if under influence of some powerful drug.

'I — s h h d d d — g o — n o w — I — w a n n t o — l e a v e — whatsssmattttter—withmyvoice—thirsty... I am thirsty...water...

can I have water—some—water,' waves of uncontrolled thirst swept over him and his head begins to swim.

'Leave? I can't let you go, Suneel Ranganathan...' the man says, 'You heard me right, you bastard. Or should I say—Mr Sonny?'

To Ranga the voice sounds as if it came from far away.

Did he say Sonny?

No one has called him by that name in so long!

'How—do you know—how—is—it—possible—who—who'ar you? What—happennnnto my tong—tongue?—whatsss—happning—to—me—' To his dismay Ranga finds that his body is unable to perform the simple action of moving his neck or even a finger.

'Mr Sonny—you were so full of arrogance that you thought no one will ever know what you did?' There is something so singularly obsessive in his gaze that Ranga is spooked.

'Who—what–why'm–I—here—want water—gimmewatrrr—' Ranganathan tries to scream loudly, but his tongue is stuck in his mouth and he can only manage a hoarse whisper.

'I told you I know your secrets, and killing and looting is another area you have shown ingenuity in... You remember the "Witch", don't you?' A belated rush of panic gripped Ranga's senses. There was a proportional coldness in his assaulter's gaze.

'Lemme—let—me—go—plss—who—who are—you?'

'That does not matter. She saw you with the little boys, didn't she? You and your friends with the little boys, she saw you—you knew that didn't you—'

The lawyer's back becomes straight and the pinprick on his neck blazes red. In his head it's all exploding in one flash like the opening of a secret box buried in quick sand with locks and fetters—

'She saw your pervert acts with the children. You killed her for that. What did you do to her, and the missing children, Mr Sonny?'

Ranganathan's mouth flaps uncontrollably and saliva drools from a corner of his lips.

'Just tell me what you did to her—I promise I will set you free, Mr Sonny.'

'In—in the field—we buried—old—woman—in the field—we buried her—in the field plss don't kill me!'

'Who ordered her rape?'

'I—had—nothing—to do with that—was the—headman—we gave—him—money—he g't his men—to—teach h'r—a lesson—she w's—threatening us—she would tell everyone she said—cut—off—her—tongue—buried—her—' Ranganathan desperately wants to feel something—anything—in his slowly mummifying body.

'What about the children? You killed them too?'

'No—no—we—didn't—kill—them—sold them—in—city—didn't—kill. Pls—listen—t'me—I c'n—make it up—to you—how much money—you—want—I'll—do—anything.'

'You can do anything? You bastard can you get her back to life? Can you get my Mother back?'

It was the boy!

The son. She had a son.

No one could possibly know. The proof was long buried and gone. A hallucination. This could not be real.

But it had been so so long ago—

He was the son. He knew about the killing and about the children…

The man does not try to stop the lawyer when he stumbles out of the Pit mad with pain and fear.

✿

A frightened scream brings the party to a halt. It is a scream of shock and outrage but mostly of indescribable horror of such proportions that those present scream in reflex. When they see Ranganathan the screams become louder. Ranganathan tips right and left and then leans against the wall gasping for breath and finally falls on his massive stomach. He struggles to get up in agony and throws up with such force that the vomit splashes at some of the guests. A spreading octopus pattern of blood soaks into the carpeted-floor. By the time the in-house doctor reaches Ranganathan, it is too late for him.

31

Molly Limaye
Sunday, 15 November
503 Glengate, Molly Limaye's apartment

It could very well turn into the day she got fired. But that's not the only reason why Molly Limaye is restless as she stands barefoot in the tiny balcony of her fifth floor apartment.

Molly is annoyed at the massive signboard an under construction building had erected right opposite her balcony last night and effectively blocking her 'three inches' of sea, her only solace when she had rented the apartment—'Sea view for the privileged few'—it announced in its advertisement for flat bookings. She is annoyed because the property agent had charged extra for the 'preferential sea-facing location' of her apartment. Betrayal of the public under the garb of progress is everywhere around her—so what if one more company does it, the cynic in her smirks.

Her neighbour calls out from the adjacent balcony, 'Molly, I wanted to talk to you, do you want a pet? My dog has given birth to—'

'I don't keep dogs. I don't keep pets.'

'You have a fish. I have seen it.'

'A fish is not the same. A dog is almost human. Feels not right to own a dog,' she said. The neighbour turned back and slammed her balcony door.

'Whatever.' Last evening her editor had dismissed her story on Medici with a derisive 'I will certainly not run stories because you feel something is wrong with making money—since when has making money become a crime? In certain civilizations this is collateral progress...'

Molly downs a scalding sip of coffee and re-scrutinizes the set of papers spread on her bed and table: an alarming report on the 'effectiveness' of the Medici's Heal drugs. The papers had been delivered again in a yellow packet by her mystery abettor. This time addressed to Dr Diaz of Medici's R&D wing is the letter by the International Institute of Clean Soil and Water accusing Medici of not paying heed to its concerns. Getting around the scientific terms had not been easy for her, but it isn't difficult to see that the nature of evidence is damning. She rereads the report for the nth time:

> *...Our findings indicate that to be stable, the beta vaccine which is used to make the Heal drug is dependant on the enzyme which is obtained from the mountain tuna. Without this key ingredient it's impossible to keep the vaccine durable. By itself the enzyme is not harmful and that pointed us in the wrong direction initially. However, the result of our new tests, are alarming as we have conveyed several times to you. The piscicides or fish poison which we suspect is being used to increase the population of the red fish has the Bayluscide derivative which is converting into a highly unstable and harmful salt.*
>
> *We have attached our detailed study and analysis of the dangerous effects of the unstable salt on the human anatomy. This active salt has the ability to cross the protective blood-brain barrier by binding with an essential amino acid that has dedicated carrier proteins for shunting it into brain cells. The salts will not show up in active form in the fish but are unstable in*

human physiologies and can lead to hair loss and skin eruptions to blindness and womb deaths. We feel it's imperative that you take into account our findings, get them tested by another independent lab by all means, but till then in the sake of public interest you should stop, immediately stop, the launch of the Heal drug. We also have worrying information that apart from Heal drugs, Medici intends to use its beta derivate in paints, diuretics, pesticides, skin creams—

Keeping aside the report, Molly picks up a novel to read—a pacy thriller. She does that often. The best solution to a problem comes to her when her mind is preoccupied with something totally different. She likes to give her mind some space of its own. One thing is clear to her. The matter now is beyond the stage of truth and lies. She decides she can no longer dismiss the evidence in front of her as some subjective dilemma addressing which would be a waste of time. The city slept in the bed of its own creation not unlike an abandoned child trapped in an opiate induced sleep. But her rational mind looks at the greed of the city with a mix of scorn and pity underlined by a feeling of betrayal and shame. It would have been so much easier to have just listened to the editor and go for that fully paid European press junket and leave this story behind. But she knows that if she lets go of this one then she would have to abandon all quixotic pretensions of wanting to do stories which mean something.

Molly picks up the pharmaceutical directory and her search ends at Group Of Companies, the body which has filed several complaints against Medici at the Regional Court of Pharma Malpractice.

32

Dorab Silva
Sunday, 15 November
Link Road, near exit 13
Case no. 55/63/2018/dineshthackray/

There is nothing more exasperating for a policeman than to feel a certain moral certainty of the guilt of a person and yet find that facts hardly bear testament to the same. There are no visible openings to get at the truth. Every point has been probed and tested. But he is running against a constant blank and his head feels stretched taut to its limit. To fob off the feeling of suffocation, Silva empties the bitter tincture into his mouth and reels back in shock from the stab in his stomach. The jolt is intense but it sobers him and banishes the haze into a remote corner of his head. His pager blinks, informing him of a ruckus at the nearby beach stretch. Some boisterous 'rainbow party' had gone out of hand and he was being directed to check out the distress call. It is 10.43 pm. What does he have to go home for anyway? Silva diverts his car towards the beach. He has heard about 'rainbow parties', the type of party where girls wear a different shade of lipstick and each proceed to give one or more men a blow job. The multiple colours left on each man's penis resembled a rainbow and the man who got all the colours first was the winner and was awarded a gift hamper. So, men ejaculate into women's mouths and wait till they get hard again. And it goes on all night. The gift hamper which awaits them at the end of their rainbow was apparently worth it. Arse, Beach and Coke, the ABC of trouble, for as long as he could remember. Both the strip bar and the tattoo bar looks empty. Except for a sick smell of stale sex, discarded drinks, a few used condoms, and some kids with glazed eyes.

'What happened here?'

'Am I in trouble, sir? A chubby girl sniffs and Silva knows its not because she is crying. 'Should you be in trouble?' Silva asks. The girl's eyes widen in fear and she squats on the sand too dead-beat to hold her own weight.

'Someone misled you I think, Mr Policeman Sir,' her boyfriend interjects.

'Really, you little punk.'

'Some boys broke bottles…some fight over a chick. But no one there now, sir,' he ends uncertainly. Silva points at the boy's penis hanging out of his pants. It has the colours of the rainbow.

'Did you also contribute to that painting?' Maybe I should take you to the slammer and you can give a live demonstration of your talent?' After questioning them for twenty minutes and putting the fear of the devil in them Silva lets them go. They are just kids trying to be old.

'Get out. Go home before I change my mind. And take this animal with you.'

By the time Silva gets out of there the lights are blinking less regularly and it is closer to dawn. Feeling terribly tired Silva yawns thickly. He has probably thought of too many things from too many different angles and all that hyper-thinking has unsettled his head. It was as if his mind had tuned to a dead channel. After a valiant attempt to organize the jumble in his head he gives up. He yawns, stretching every muscle in his face, and catches his reflection on the back view mirror, the skin around his eyes is turning blue. His body feels on fire and each movement is excruciatingly painful. He stumbles out of the car and hits first head on the door but the world is a blur. In this near-paralyzed state a patrol car discovers him several hours later, stretched on the road, near his car.

Recovery room, D-Path Hospital
Room no. 3
Patient name: ACP Dorab Silva

It was a lovely dream. He knew it had to be a dream because he was sitting with his wife in it and the sun was blazing through the dusty almond trees along a warm riverbank. They were sitting like tired old folks listening happily to a train's whistle and laughing at old jokes. And then the train leaves track and runs over her, and Silva wakes up as if from death.

'Well, what do you know, boss! I guess hell ain't prepared for a stubborn old dog like you!' Gouda's voice is full of relief.

'What the hell are you talking about, motherfucker?' Silva's voice is a harsh whisper.

'Good to see you too. Back from shadowland!'

'What happened?' Silva mumbles.

'The boys found you crashed on the road and halfway to China!' They got scared when you didn't wake up. When I reached and saw that on your head I called the doctor immediately.' Gouda points at Silva's head. There is a bluish purple bruise on his temple and his right cheekbone is swollen, probably from a fall.

A doctor peers into his wound. Even in his state Silva recognizes Dr Das, a well-known toxicologist. Dr Das pours some hydrogen peroxide into his palm and slaps it into the gash like an after-shave.

It is a painful sting and he has to put his hand firmly on his mouth to keep himself from crying out. When the pain starts to fade a little, the doctor soaks cotton balls with more peroxide and holds it against the wound. With a forcep he retrieves something, smells it gingerly and frowns.

'Hmmm. This is unusual,' says Dr Das with a worrying look.

'What happened to me?' demands Silva, trying to keep from losing consiousness.

'You will know soon. Keep your hand still.' Dr Das's reputation as a criminological scientist is formidable. 'That will do,' Dr Das said as he transfers his precious find to a plastic wrapper.

'In a few hours I may be able to give you some information. Before you go off to a long sleep due to the antibiotics I have given you, I have one question, where did you go last?'

'I was at the beach—' Silva struggles to recall, 'before that I had gone to meet Neville Valentine.'

'Valentine? Should we take him in—' interrupts Gouda.

'Don't be an idiot, Gouda. There is nothing on him—his lawyers will be all over the department.'

'Boss, I thought you would like to know, but we found the body of a Medici lawyer by the name of Suneel Ranganathan. Doctors at the morgue say they haven't even seen anything like it—apparently his penis burst, leaked blood like a burst water cannon. They found some suspicious substance in his blood, it is being tested in the lab—' Gouda drones on but Silva is past hearing, having drifted into a deep sleep.

33

Binky Mendez
Sunday, 15 November
Apartment No. 52, Verona (Building facing Molly Limaye's apartment)

It is the eleventh day of Binky Mendez's noiseless surveillance of Molly Limaye's apartment. And he is doing it with the intensity of a man for whom the shining sun has lost meaning. Kimmy's betrayal and Molly's snooping around has plummeted Binky's distrust in people to psychotically low levels. So, when he had received the call from one of his informers he feared the worst.

'What is it?'

'Just take it easy. I'm going through the pictures taken by the cameras we installed near Molly's apartment.'

'And?'

'You can see our man in the camera. I will send you the image on WhatsApp….he had dark glasses and a cap on. But his cap came off for a bit so—'

Binky's phone beeps to indicate it has received an image file.

'So, do you know him from somewhere? Do you know him?' said the informer.

'No, he is averting his face from the camera. You moron, he knows it's there.'

Binky is still on the phone when the man zooms into his line of view. Clutching a large yellow-coloured manilla envelope the man is entering Molly's building. Binky positions himself near the gaps in the kitchen railing from where he can get a clearer view. There is something about his body language that makes Binky start. Face firmly covered by a hood, the man lingers in front of the locked door and then leans over and throws another package into Molly's balcony and leaves. There is no sense of urgency in the man's movements. Binky races to another room for a better view. He spots him below on the street. The street light casts a reddish-yellow light from above, and from his vantage point Binky can make out his profile. When the man turns his head Binky feels he is looking straight into the eyes set above cheekbones so prominent that they look like they had been chiseled by a knife. Binky gasps in shock.

It was… but it couldn't be… just couldn't!
Was it Boy?

Binky re-focuses the field glasses and almost drops them again. He is not mistaken.

It was definitely BOY!

Binky Mendez watches Boy remove his jacket and carefully place it in a polythene bag in the back bonnet of his motorcycle and drive away.

What could the explanation be for the deceit which is staring at his face? He aims to get to the bottom of the buisness right now before informing Valentine.

34

Neville Valentine
Sunday, 15 November
Medici Studio

***Healers*/Scene 7/Act 3/Lines 65–80/Time 2.05 p.m.**

'I offer them escape—I am Roy—they will do anything I say—I am their God…who are you? How dare you question me—'

Valentine said his dialogues in a tone that is meant to subjugate his co-star, a young debutant.

'No one has the right to question me, least of all you—And—I… eh… Fuck. Fuck. I cannot remember a blasted fucking word!' Beads of sweat appear on Valentine's forehead as he forces his mind to recall 'Roy's' dialogues. But his mind is blank.

'I don't want that actor to be in the same frame as me. He is stealing my light,' he complains to Aslam.

'But, Mr Valentine,' Aslam takes a thoughtful pause before he can summon up a response, 'that actor is 'Roy's friend. The scene is okayed by Ms Rani Nadda. I have no say in the matter.'

'I don't care. The bastard is stealing my light,' Valentine complains childishly and Aslam presses his throbbing temple.

Healers/Scene 7/Act 3/Lines 24-40/Time 2.22 p.m.

'*... Are you scared of the dark? I am not. You know what she told me when she left me—she said I am too dark for her. How dare she leave me like some jaded whore? You know what she said—eh—I—*'

'Fuck. Who the fuck wrote these lines? They are impossible to remember!'

It is the fifth attempt to finish the shooting of the final scene of *Healers*.

'This is insane! I can't remember my fucking lines...'

Anger seems to pierce the fibre of the Superstar's sanity. Such is the intensity of the rage which lashes inside him that he cannot stop his hands from shaking. But if a doctor were to take his critical readings at that moment the only indication of the extreme events taking place inside him would be the icy dampness of his upper body and manic heartbeat.

'That's okay. Let's take a break for an hour,' a desperate Aslam darts worried glances in Valentine's direction, who seems trapped in a trance.

'They make fun of me, Boy—I know what they say behind my back...old man on the brink.' Valentine holds his head in his hands and moans.

'Don't worry, mister—I have created this ointment which will calm your skin.' Boy applies the contour paint with furious brush-strokes smoothening wrinkes on his face and manages to give a healthy bronze colour and tone to Valentine's skin.

'Your paints can't help me, Boy...no one can help me I feel—even my nights are damned.'

Valentine recalls the dream he'd had the night before—it had begun beautifully, an intoxicating girl with slanted eyes and golden skin and lips like rubies—she was telling him something—her bright eyes, rosebud breasts and glowing young skin filled him with a wild sense of delightful freedom. He saw himself fucking her—but when he touched her forehead, her skin turned icy and her face changed to an older woman with long brown hair which was filled with blood, he woke up with a pounding heart. The dream's force had held him in its grip, not willing to let go even now when he was wide awake.

'Help me, Boy…can you stop these demons who live in my head. I am scared they are becoming a part of me. I don't know who I fight now!' he wails.

Healers/Scene 7/Act 3/Lines 96-110/Time 4.55 p.m.

It is the eighth attempt to finish the shooting of the final scene of *Healers*. Valentine's hair looks limp and his eyes are dull stones sinking into his alabaster face. The shooting has been slowed down to a snail's pace.

'My skin that you love so much. What does it do? Keeps me in. Keeps you out. I open a window and all the madness flows in. And out. It is seeping out of me from all sides leaking like some ectoplasm. I have to stem it. Hold it in. Hold my hell in. Before, there was nothing left of me. Nothing except a mad thought…'

At this point, Valentine stops speaking. His face is in a trance, his skin ice cold and yet he sweats profusely. The rage in his head has reached a point of singularity. It weighs a tonne and it cannot be contained. A part of him imagines shadows unpinning themselves from dark corners one by one and moving towards him in a single file. A crazy thought seizes Valentine—if only he can somehow transfer the scourge gnawing at him from inside to someone— anyone—a sacrifice? He has to make an offering to the demon to feed on, so he can be absolved of more suffering. Before anyone realizes, Valentine seizes the junior actor's neck and throws the stunned boy on a couch. Still holding his white neck in a pincer grip, he hammers the other man's face, his ring cutting deep gaping red craters. Air hissed into the wounds and warm blood trickles down and there is complete commotion as men try to separate the two. The young actor fights to break free, but Valentine does not let go.

'I will not allow anyone—will not allow anyone—no one—to make me feel lesser!'

'Aiekkkk—nooo—stop stop—LET HIM GO—for God's sake—someone get him off! Are you in your senses, man?' Aslam yells in panic. At that moment Valentine looks up and catches his reflection in a mirror, but the play of sunlight tricks his senses and what stares back is a thickly modelled monochrome of a bony skull framed to perfection, a gilded skeleton.

'Who is that! Do I look like a monster—stop! Don't switch the lights off!' Valentine releases the bruised man and lunges towards a petrified set hand.

'Mr Valentine! I am only trying to switch off...'

꽃

'Don't steal my light—go, get out, GET OUT ALL OF YOU!'

The motionless sun sinks into the waters of Dambi behind the N.V mansion and turns into a molten plate of fire. Valentine is lying still. He does not feel the cold breeze rise from an open window and carve out gooseflesh into his skin.

'You must be thinking I am mad, Boy. But when the lights went off I panicked—'

'Mister, you will be fine soon.'

'How will I be well? Despair follows me like a mad dog... I'd sell my soul for one night's sleep.'

'Trust me, you will be fine soon.'

'No. I feel worse. Worse than today morning. Worse than a minute ago. Where the fuck is Binky Mendez when I need him?'

'You will be fine, mister. Have patience.'

'Patience for what, you fool? Are you even listening to a word I am saying?' The bedrail rattles harshly when he grips it to stand upright.

'Help—what's happening to me—why can't I move?' Valentine feels a stab of pain in his chest and for some reason his eyes keep snapping shut as if painted by invisible glue. He blinks several times but the world had distorted and darkness has engulfed him.

*

'Why is it so dark here? Who's there—Boy, is that you?'

Valentine wakes up in a crouching position. As the sunrays stream through the cut glass of a high window into cold slivers of dusty yellow, he gets up and wipes the urine stuck to his groin and inner thighs. He is shivering and cold and had let his bladder go, feeling helpless in damp piss—dirty and ashamed. The metal of the rail was cool as he gripped it to haul himself up. Halfway up, a near-blinding visceral pain ripped through his body. Every gut and muscle in his body seems to contort into a tight knot as he waits for some diabolical menace to acquire face.

'My name is not Boy. It is Akhouri, mister. I cannot tell you how long have I waited to see that look on your face.'

35

Binky Mendez
Sunday, 15 November
Suit Number 10, Transit camp, State entry road,
(Boy's apartment)

Binky Mendez's entry into Boy's tiny apartment is without mishap, mainly because he had already confirmed that Boy was with Valentine before breaking into his flat. The thought that Boy—the man of science who would spend hours in his lab, not emerging for days sometimes, to prepare healing balms for Valentine—was involved in deceit is driving him mad with fury and he wants to get to the bottom of it. The first thing he notices is how sparsely the room is furnished. The white acoustic tiles look yellow with the spillage of chemicals and the brown textured rug near the table rested compacted by extensive use. Under the low ceiling stood rows of long tables, like in a chemistry lab, scribbled walls and shelves stacked with phials of resins and powders in clouded jars and crystals wrapped in protective glazes and a strong smell of vinegar and saltpeter burns his nostrils. The more Binky Mendez thinks of how they met the more he feels convinced that it was Boy who had found him and not the other way round.

The first time Binky had met Boy was almost two years ago when he was admitted to the Medici hospital after an AC duct had exploded and left him with severe burns on his face, neck and chest. The cell damage was so serious that after the medical tests he was put on the waiting list for skin grafting, along with a regular dosage of Konakion, Inderal and Spironolacton. The pain was so much that he could not sleep for more than one or two hours every night. Meditation, hypnosis, self-suggestion, sleep-techniques nothing had helped. Binky's tissues had collapsed and gangrene was setting in, he had been awake for five days and had had several psychotic episodes. He had voluntarily admitted himself to a private hospital. One day, when he was almost out of his mind with pain he had found Boy next to his bed. Short and lean with thin hair, a high forehead, prominent cheekbones and pale, almost translucent, skin—Boy had claimed to be a trained healer studying to be a doctor. And there was no reason to doubt him when Binky woke up the following morning without screaming from pain. The hospital called it a miracle when his name was taken off the skin transplant list. He had readily accepted the propitious meeting with Boy as a happy accident and offered him a job, a house and a motorcycle (Boy had refused a car). Never in his dream had he imagined anything amiss. There was never any need to probe his credentials as a healer, he was so extraordinarily talented. There was something that had struck a chord—like the way he would light up when left alone to work in his lab and his odd disconnection with the world. Of course if he had probed he would have found out that there was no medical-trainee by his name in the institute he had mentioned. And even the company he had said he had interned with did not exist.

Feeling drained, Binky sits down on the only clean chair in the room. Next to the assembled desktop of a basic kind, which clever students with scarce funds put together using screwdrivers and pliers, he spots the innocuous-looking papers. Sheafs of scribbled notes, summaries, jottings and print outs, and it seems that Boy has performed a triage of sorts on the stack of papers. Binky looks around the lab for a table to lay the sheets on and study them more closely. He gets more and more baffled as he reads and re-reads the sheets. Photocopies of private correspondence between Medici and other organizations, Neville Valentine's private property bond listings, contractual letters, cheque details and even land holding details of Suneel Ranganathan—meticulously procured by Boy. He notices Ranga's name has been circled several times so hard that the nib has gone through the paper. Binky Mendez's nails dig into his flesh till angry red welts appear as if the pain could replace the boiling rage in his heart.

What is his diabolical plan?

Binky knows he cannot let Boy know his deceit has been discovered—at least not until his real motive is identified. But he must warn Valentine before Boy does any further harm. With his mission clear in his head, Binky rushes out of the house. In his haste Binky fails to see the speeding car coming from the other side until it is too late. It rams into him with such a speed that he is thrown up into the sky and caught mid-air by a speeding truck from the wrong side. The truck vanishes in a dusty haze along with the car which is being driven by Kimmy White. It is already too late for Binky Mendez, whose cerebral cortex has blown like a tyre and he is already drowning in his own blood. Death comes in a short black supernova of pain. He is gone even before he hits the ground.

36

Akhouri and Valentine
Monday, 16 November
Day 1 of captivity
Basement Cellar, 555 Neverland

'The dose makes the poison, if you ask me, mister. On you latex worked admirably well, like skin in the way it lent itself to your body—an unpenetrable barrier to healing, constantly gouging out goodness from your flesh—of course now it is too late,' Akhouri says.

'I cannot feel my skin—burninggg—Boy—Akhouri—whoever you are, why am I hot when my skin is freezing—' Valentine screams and rubs his face as if trying to get some warmth into his icy skin.

'That would be the latex you admire for its shine, with some tetrodoxin from red fish to paralyse you. But your nerves are intact—so you can feel all the pain in the world.' On hearing his words, Valentine's eye sockets expand as if his head is trying to turn into a skull.

'Mister, you often asked me about its sheen—it is a liquid colloid of quicksilver, commonly known as mercury. It gave your skin the lustre that camera loved. The problem is—it invades the skin if left on for long periods…fuses with your body—never going away until you die. Merciless, unstoppable. But for me that was never a problem. It was the solution.'

'Have you gone mad? What do you want from me, Boy?'

'That does not matter now. Have you forgotten again? My name is Akhouri. But that too doesn't matter.'

'Akhouri...who is making you do this? Who is paying you—?'

'No one. At least no one you know, mister.'

'Listen Akhouri—I am not well.... I have a lot of money... I will give you all of it... I will forget this ever happened, just help—help me—no one needs to know what your crime...'

'My crime?' Akhouri laughs. But the laughter does not reach his eyes.

'I have done nothing to you!' Valentine screams.

'That's why it's so important for you to remember, mister. You know my mother gave me my name, it means the unknown. I suggest you do not get so agitated. It increases the temperature of the body. The latex I have covered you with remains in elemental state at room temperature—harmless like rubber, but as the body heats up it converts to liquid. And will sink into the skin faster and into your brain and blood. It has already been working on you—the mood changes—the anger for no apparent reason, and the nightmares! The tremors...the slurring...the panic attacks during the day? You are already in stage two. Soon you will enter the painful third stage—soft gums, teeth will loosen, the sores...'

'Oh my god.' Valentine looks pitiful.

'The only question you should be asking is how much time you have. '

'I can't feel my skin!'

'Why should I give a damn? You never did. I will leave you on one condition. That you remember what you did. C'mon, that's a small thing to ask of you, mister?

Valentine looks at the picture Akhouri is holding.

'For Gods's sake I don't know her...who the fuck is she?'

'Hmmm. I won't worry about that. You will remember everything soon. Because the chemicals in my medicines are breaking down the walls in your head...soon the past and present will meet and then—then you will beg to forget. But I promise my medicines won't kill you, mister.'

'You can't keep me here forever, you bastard—Binky will find me!'

'Pray for that Valentine. But that will be a waste of time. For by the look of you I think it's my demons who will find you first. Till then you have your favourite toys to play with.'

37

Akhouri and Valentine
Wednesday, 18 November
Day 3 of Captivity
Basement cellar, SSS Neverland

He is not having a nightmare. He is really captive in the basement of his own house. His dungeon, his labour of love has become his prison. Valentine knows that there is no way for anyone to find him behind the masterfully constructed soundproof walls, unless they knew where to look.

Valentine has lost the sense of time because of the basement's darkness. He has lost the sense of touch because of his icy fingers and toes. Minutes turn to hours and days, and the beginning of loss of hope as he waits for death or something worse. During the night, the chains hanging from the walls rattle, they have tasted blood before and he imagines the steel of the chain cutting into his flesh and shackles binding his feet and in his overactive imagination the equipment of his pleasure turn to instruments of torture.

When Akhouri informs him that Binky is dead, he is stupefied. Binky had been his last hope. He would have known where to look. The confined air around him is bloated with his fluids desolate with his dirt. It smells of some vile carbolic emulsion. He has lost track of the number of times he has lost the contents of his stomach. Time has stopped, he feels. Or maybe its flowing both ways. Was it an hour ago, a day, weeks since his world melted down.

38

Akhouri and Valentine
Friday, 20 November
Day 5 of Captivity
Basement cellar, SSS Neverland

Rats wake him more frequently now. Last night he caught one with its teeth dug in his thigh. He pulled it out and threw it against the wall. It scurried away into the shadows staring back, its half-eaten feast. It had patient eyes and Valentine knows it will be back for more. He does not want to be alone anymore. He is increasingly terrified of being alone.

'Did I tell you Mr Sonny is dead too?' Akhouri tells him matter of factly.

'Sonny...' Valentine closes his eyes tightly as if trying to prevent memory from escaping the innermost corner of his head.

'Yes. Suneel Ranganathan. But you know him as Mr Sonny too—' Valentine's weakened body could barely move. 'I don't know anything... I think—'

'Your mind has gotten feeble. It will not be able to mask the truths anymore?' Akhouri's eyes were two menacing holes of such dark venom that Valentine's heart slams in his chest and he starts retching and sobbing. Attempts to impose order on his thoughts are useless and his mind stands on the verge of becoming a bowl of loose gruel, a flawed container.

That night in his dream shadows unpin themselves from the

walls and when he opens his eyes he sees her in the dungeon with him…and she smiles…and he wonders… How is it possible? He starts screaming when the girl moves towards him.

39

Akhouri and Valentine
Sunday, 22 November
Day 7 of Captivity
Basement cellar, 555 Neverland

It is not possible. It had to be a nightmare. With a weak movement his palms pressed heavily on his lids as if to block bloody memories and he wakes up with a scream. But the spectre infesting his dreams is standing next to his bed. Could memories acquire flesh and bones till they became entitities, Valentine wonders. It is dark but he can see clearly. The girl is young with slanted eyes and golden skin. She takes his face in his hands and shoves her tongue inside his open mouth. Her tongue tastes of sandoz sticks and spliffs and her breath reeks of weed and marijuana. He wants to shake her off but her grip is too strong. It is impossible for him to sifter out or clear his mind. He wants to tell her to go away but not a sound comes out of his mouth. He remains a mute spectator as the section bent on dragging out black memories from the depths of his mind works overtime. The spectre's robust face starts sinking inside its own skull and bones jut out rapidly tearing through her skin and she is now an older woman, with translucent skin and coal black eyes and long brown hair. Someone screams 'Witch!' and it all comes to him, in no order of importance, like a stuck camera flashing all the truths at one go, and he just a captive spectator. He knew what's going to happen next because he is reliving it. For the first time, the vast blankness which had shuttered his heart slides and he truly understands the horror of what had transpired years ago.

Akhouri's voice floats into his sleep deprived head.

'My medicine is inside you—it flows in your blood, is a part of your flesh enveloped in the warmth of your tissue. It has stayed in you long enough and reached every part of your body with the blood flow guided by your heartbeat. Soon it will be too late. I can still help you. Tell me what you did and why?'

A strangled sob escapes Valentine's throat. 'I never wanted to kill her—thought they would only scare her—so she would keep her mouth shut.'

'Keep her mouth shut about what Ranga was doing with the little boys?'

'He said she was bad news—she kept saying the company had poisoned the waters. And then she saw the children—Sonny had the missing children with him—she threatened she would tell everyone—I was scared!'

'You let them kill her because you got richly paid and just looked the other way?' Akhouri spat out the words.

'No—not for the money—not just the money,' Valentine moans.

'She had seen me too with the children,' he says dully. 'It was in a mad, mad moment—I swear I was never going to do it again—I have never done it again—but she saw me. She was so angry…she won't listen to me…said she would tell the world I was also apart of it. But I wasn't like that!' Valentine sobs pathetically. Akhouri listens in silence.

'Imagine how it would have looked! I would have lost everything. I had just signed films…my life was just starting… no one would have worked with me if the word had gotten out!

What could I have done! It was so long ago…'

'There is no difference between Suneel Ranganathan and you and Medici feeding on everything that was good, destroying lives…' Akhouri says finally.

'Please—help me—don't leave me here—I don't want to be alone—'

'She didn't deserve to die. Those children didn't deserve what happened to them. Damn you, Mister Valentine! Damn you!'

His eyes reflecting unimaginable horror, Akhouri looks at Valentine one last time and leaves.

Valentine is frozen in deathly silence like a caged animal. He is scared to make a noise. He is scared to sleep. He doesn't want her to come back. His eyes dart into the dark corners of the empty room. He sees her again.

The Witch of the Dune.

Closer.

Clearer.

Neville Valentine will never know the precise moment his world dissolved permanently into a slush.

40

Dorab Silva
Sunday, 22 November
Recovery room, D-Path Hospital
Case no. 55/63/2018/dineshthackray/

Dr Das is fond of saying that only with shrewd reasoning from effect to cause one can ever get to the truth. There are many great scientists in the world and many great detectives—he exhibits characteristics of both.

'It's alarming! Unusual!' the doctor cannot conceal his excitement.

'I am not feeling that bad,' Silva says.

'Have you looked into the mirror, boss? Here take a look…'

The strange yellow rings at the corner of his eyes looks like shit leaking out and when he smells it, he gags.

'See what we mean?'

'By amazing I mean the substance found in you—its nature is alarming.'

'You were poisoned,' Gouda comes to the point.

'Poisoned?' Silva waits for the men to make sense.

'There are two important things I will now convey to you based on my analysis. First regarding your condition: you were poisoned. But there was little erosion of the stomach tissue and limited dehydration. The good thing is whoever poisoned you, assuming such was the case, did not intend to kill you. The intention it appears was only to put you out of action for a while. I have sent it for further analysis to the toxicology lab. Although I am more or less sure of its nature.'

'But who would poison me?'

'Malafide intention cannot be ruled out considering your line of work. It could also have been ingested inadvertently except this is a very particular Piperidine complex. It has to be made by an expert in these matters, a doctor or chemist or at the very least a talented druggist. You need remarkable pharmaceutical knowledge to not overdo the ingredients which can lead to severe hallucination and worse. Quite rare this colloid derivative is, the poison I mean.'

'Simplify for God's sake!' Silva's eyes are yellowish.

'Well, there is nothing simple about it. This poison which has been found on your person is a sort of a reverse biocide. In science, biocides are known as life-sustaining, they help in nurturing, perpetuate balance of nature. But this poison is reverse, an Omnicide—a mimic, closest to what is called an Organic Death Particle. It's believed to lead to the irreversible destruction of a living organism.'

'Death particle? Mimic?'

'To put it simply, mimic is a "bad" particle—reverse of a biocide which is supposed to be "good"—mimic, inverted in all its properties! Mimics target the same metabolic pathways, shut it down or makes it toxic. I have not seen something like this used as a weapon—and this is not the place, I can safely say, I expected to find something like it!'

'You found this weird stuff in me? It is impossible—'

'This weird stuff is not as rare as you think. For instance, the herbicide 2,4-dichlorophenoxyacetic acid is a mimic of a plant growth hormone, which causes uncontrollable growth leading to the death of the plant. On humans and animals it will be ineffective, totally harmless. It could just pass out with urine or sweat unless the body has been injected with a receptor hormone, then it is uncontrollable.'

'But where do you get it from? Who makes this stuff?' Silva is baffled and Dr Das tries to simplify the information as much as he can.

'Biocides are synthetic, but a class of natural biocides can be derived from bacteria plants, even fish. Poison lends itself most conveniently to a good murder with it's worm-like stealth. Of all the methods to murder, this would be the most painful and cruel one. This is the probably the only way to murder someone and get off scot-free. Easy to administer and if you do your homework well, there is no dearth of poisons which leave no apparent mark.'

'And this "mimic" has got something to do with this yellow shit leaking out of my eyes, then?'

'Good deduction. The skin as you must have noticed has become yellow and patchy—in the area of cheek, ears, lips…it's like you rubbed into it. The yellow will go. With the treatment I am giving you it will come out in the urine because you are still alive, might burn a bit. Had you been dead your eyes would secrete this for days. Little pearls around the eyes just like so,' the doctor made a soft ring around Silva's yellow-rimmed eyes and brought it cautiously towards his nose.

'You said there are two things. What is the second thing?'

'That bit is of far more important consequences to Thackeray's murder case. The poison we found on you is of same nature which we found in Mr Thackray's system.'

The doctor points to a picture of Dinesh Thackray's corpse. He zooms into the area around the dead man's empty-looking eyes. The colour of his iris was all mixed up and it looked messy like someone has defecated into them and bits were streaming off his lids which were rimmed with little round marbles of dull yellow. Of course the dose given to Thackray was a killer concentration as compared to you. And that explains these yellow crystals—Thackray's corpse had been leaking them for days.

'Both of us were poisoned the same way?' Silva cannot believe what he is hearing.

'Perhaps you got plain unlucky. Perhaps you got too close to the killer. Who knows? That's for you to find out. There's one more thing. The extract needed to make this is obtained from certain leaves—maguey—found in some of the Northeastern hills. Their flowers have different smells—multi-fragranted. There is a practise in certain countries to administer this complex for healing purposes. To cure a kind raging madness or extreme violence. Sort of a medicinal lobotomy. So, its results depend on how much and in which form you take it—'

The doctor shows another picture and Silva peers at it with renewed interest. 'We compared some of Thackray's old pictures of when he was young and alive to some of his recent ones from just before his death. The distinctive yellowish tinge in his eyes, the unnatural red swelling started to appear a year ago…so whoever was administering this to him, started with little doses. Little enough to not kill but to start the decay of his body. It's as if someone wanted him to suffer before he was killed,' Dr Das explains.

'But how do we find out who is responsible? It could be anyone.'

'You know here we might just be lucky. The thing is this poison is hard to use. Not very stable. The complex just breaks apart easily, so most people need a stabilizer. The thing is that the ingredients to make the stabilizer are stocked at only at a few drugstores. I explained the same to Mr Gouda and he already has his team working on it.'

'We are looking into it. The boys are talking to every drugstore on this side and the other. Boss, are you okay? Doctor, is he fine? He looks like he is going to faint…' Gouda asks worriedly.

Silva's eyes widen unnaturally, his body is strangely still. He feels the familiar rush of excitement that one feels when on the verge of discovering something very crucial, as if the truth is finally out in the open. He folds his hands together again on the table top as if to calm himself. In a puzzling move, he selects a particular photograph. Breathing heavily, he compares the photograph to the pictures on the computer screen as if solving a photo puzzle. Singling another one out, he repeats the process. After a while, he straightens himself and his eyes glitter with deduction.

'Pictures always tell a story. This is a very interesting story—'

Silva zooms past Thackray's face and focuses on the arm casually resting on Hiri's breast and stops at the cufflink on that arm. His gaze flickers sideways at his laptop as he types in a few words and hits 'Search'. Immediately Valentine is up on the screen, smiling in scores of pictures. He saves some of them on the desktop and uses the amplification tool to enlarge the customized logo mark and compares it with the mark on the cufflink. There is no mistake. The mark is identical to the engraving on the cufflink, miniscule twin snakes entwined in a special way to make a tiny '**nv**'.

So, Valentine had not been avoiding looking at the girl's face as Silva had imagined at the time. The man was probably busy looking across at the incriminating piece of accessory damning him!

One always remembers that moment which changes the flow of a case and Silva feels certain he is closest to that point than he has been yet in this mystery. There were still too many unanswered questions. Questions like why had Dinesh Thackray hidden this photograph? Perhaps he was using it to threaten Valentine, maybe to make him back off from his daughter? Maybe Valentine did not like the ultimatum or threat. So did the Superstar have something to do with Thackray's death? What about the woman Hiri herself? Her death was quite a coincidence? Maybe the woman had found a way to blackmail Valentine? But that seemed unlikely, he thought, remembering her condition when he last met her. The door flies open at that moment and the silence in the room is broken. Gouda's man has some important news.

'Speak!' Silva commands.

'Boss, I had dispatched teams to the selected stores and you will never guess who our Mr Busyfingers is!'

'Tell me!'

'Our team made contact with a druggist who informed us about an unusual amount of sale of the ingredients since last six months. Well, the orders were placed in Valentine's assistant Binky Mendez's name. But that's not the only thing. The reports have come in on Ranga—and guess what?'

'Poison?'

'Punctured in the back. A particularly nasty poison spread so rapidly that it tore his tissues and muscles. The pressure inside his body built up to such a degree that he burst into himself. All gum and goo in under an hour—skin the most bizarre shade of yellow like he shat inside himself!'

'Mr Busyfingers again?' offers Dr Das thoughtfully.

'But why is Binky not in for questioning?'

'The thing is he died in a freak accident.'

'Question his boss Valentine—.

'That's the weird thing. He has been missing for almost a week now. Medici reported his disappearence. He was working in their show it seems. No one knows where the Superstar is. Some of his friends say he could have gone somewhere on his own so the headquarters has not declared an alert yet. But the word is that it will be declared by tomorrow if he doesn't show up.'

'You are telling me all this now?' Silva digests the latest information.

'Boss, you were out for almost a week—in any case you were in no condition to help and—'

'What about the goddam studio—wasn't he doing Medici's show—? Did you question them?'

'At the moment, the studio is not willing to say anything except that they have no clue. Boss, no one has a clue. It's like Valentine has vanished into this air.'

'Shut up, Gouda. No one vanishes into thin air. There is only one place where we can find a clue,' Silva said.

41

Monday, 23 November
Case no. 10/49/2018/nevillevalentine/

Search Operations, Neverland, South City

The police search helicopter circles overhead the Neverland neighbourhood. Dozens of law enforcement officers are seen carrying out multiple search operations for Superstar Neville Valentine. Police teams are going door-to-door, speaking with residents, officers in boats and on horseback have combed the river Dambi and the wooded riverside park where Valentine was last seen by a witness shortly after he left the Medici Studio for his home.

On Sunday, the police divers had taken to the river with a grim mission armed with propane heaters, scuba tanks, step ladders, heavy ropes and tools, as a team of divers assembled on the river. The seven-day search has yielded few clues and even fewer answers as to what has become of the missing star. More than 370 tips have been called in since the police launched the official alert on Monday for the missing actor. According to the police none of the tips have proved concrete nor helped to start a point of search but all hypotheses are being looked at.

The SSP of South City, D.G. Karanth, has admitted to the media that they do not know at this point if a criminal hand is involved or not, but they 'cannot exclude that hypothesis'. Police in a statement posted on Twitter late Tuesday asked people to 'stay vigilant and report any information regarding Valentine to 911' and a police statement has been issued.

Press Release

After 7.30 p.m. the seventh day's search operations have been wound up. The police search parties will continue to hunt for the missing actor. The search will be expanded to cover an even larger area of the Dambi Lake and kayakers will be recruited to join the efforts. Over a period of time, the Press/Electronic media has been sharing information with regard to the case FIR No. 10/49/2018 dated 18.01.2018 registered in Police Station, South City. The law and investigation agency is in the process of completion of investigation. However, for the last couple of days a certain section of print/electronic media has published/ broadcast information/reports shared on social media as well, which are far away from the truth. Constrained by this reportage it is to place on record that it is not yet confirmed or certain as to whether Mr Valentine fell into the part of the river behind his house, or if he met with a mishap elsewhere. The search team has combed the area further downstream towards the forest but with the high tide this morning, it is increasingly uncertain where the missing actor might be if he fell into the river. Special officers are assisting the detectives in canvassing the area, interviewing people and looking for surveillance videos.

The Medici Studio is meanwhile offering a ₹20 lakh reward for Valentine's safe return. The NV Fan Club has pledged an additional ₹15 lakh for the safe return of the star. The police say the search is becoming harder with each passing day and they are now seeking the help of federal investigators to join the investigation.

42

Monday, 23 November
555 Neverland, Neville Valentine's bungalow
Case no. 55/63/2018/dineshthackray/

Silva swallows a Migraleve Pink to jam the waves of pain but his head still hurts from the painful blowbacks in his body.

'Boss, we could have waited till tomorrow. You are still looking like shit.'

'Gouda, pay more attention to searching.'

'It would help if we knew what we are looking for, boss. This is a complete waste of time. Every inch scanned twice over. There is no clue. Valentine has vanished into thin air and we still don't know a thing.'

'Grown men don't just disappear. Unless they want to. Especially if they happen to be superstars.' Silva's voice is dull. An air of baffled futility hangs around him. The overpowering rancid smell pervading in the place makes it difficult for Silva to concentrate. The previous search team had left a window open and inadvertently allowed the day's storm and heavy dust to enter like an unwelcome guest, toppling artifacts and chairs.

'Boss, maybe he left on his yatch to some unknown destination—men like him don't worry about hours they need to clock to make pension.' Gouda sulks.

'Shut up. Just pray for a hot lead. This smell is making me sick.'

'My off hours too. I'm billing overtime, boss.'

With its expensive mahogany paneling and gold pilasters the place is a complete contrast to the bare white walls of Valentine's studio chamber he had visited and Silva wonders if this is how bipolar disorder manifests itself in the stinking rich.

Intricately woven pashmina cushions with filigree work on its border are strewn about casually in the silver Louise Quinze bathroom. The pashmina carpets feel butter smooth and Silva is aware that each little rug can pay the mortgage on his house for the next five years. The bathroom is filled with obnoxiously expensive accoutrements.

'What's this…a guilded shitter?' Gouda laughs, 'Mister Superstar uses scented coloured toilet paper to keep his hole smelling like a daisy!? I would imagine he would not drop his brick on nothing less than 24K!'

'Original carbon fibre too! Freaking shit will be around longer than us—good enough to piss though!' Silva decides to eliminate the can of soda he had unwisely consumed before coming. Pissing the yellow fluid with one eye open, he frowns like a man who has exhausted all ideas.

'The smell! What the fuck is this smell. You know, boss, I read on Google that in olden days prostitutes would grow stuff and mix plant elixirs in their oils so that their customers would come back—sort of body drugs—good enough to kill and probably finished a quite a few unpaying sods…'

'Shit. Fuck.'

'You are making me nervous, boss…'

'That smell—'

'What smell?' Gouda is just about able to keep pace.

'I know where I smelled it before!' Silva said excitedly.

'Smelled what, boss?'

Silva's mind is racing as he tries to place the sweetly rancid smell in the house. It smells exactly like the poison which had made him sick.

'The smell is stronger in that direction—muskier—definitely coming from there,' Silva has a frantic look about him as he heads towards Valentine's private chamber. Gouda is unnerved by the intensity with which his boss is sniffing the air.

The private chamber is exceptionally large with herring bone hardwood flooring, capacious book cases, large bronze and glass doors. Nothing seems to be out of place but his head feels hot. Like his senses are trying to tell him something which his mind is not being able to interpret. The minimalistic walls look incongruous against fresco-covered ceiling and he thinks that's odd because across the mansion, the ornate walls are framed in the expensive cornices. But this particular wall has a pronounced raised pargeting of hardened plasterwork. Silva has seen similar arrangements during the construction of hidden cabinets or secret rooms. In an agitated way, Silva looks about, touching, feeling, exploring the room till finally in frustration he bangs and kicks a few things. He must have touched a hidden spring mechanism, because the thickly carved wall slowly rumbles outwards revealing a cosy blue zone hidden from the outside world. The two men are absolutely mysified as they walk through it into a sturdy staircase which seems to have been built from inside a tree and corkscrewed downwards to a basement into something like a secret dungeon. The structure is designed in a way that it made it impossible to get there unless one actually knows of its existence. Inside, the air is thick with the sweet, rancid smell.

'We would be directly under the outer garage,' Silva said his breath coming fast. On the left is the entrance to another part of the dungeon. They have to hold on to the walls so that the stench does not knock them over. It is gloomy and dark, and their torches make restless swinging arcs bathing them in rippling shadows till Gouda finds the light switch. They are not prepared for what they see, a built in tank-sized custom-made Pierce Arrow bar, a sparkling wall size LCD TV perched atop a massive dark veneer bureau and a huge assortment of bondage toys, props, wall shackles, spanking benches, chains, whips and canes, riding crops and nipple clampers, bottles of lube, blindfolds, and various other accessories. A host of pleasure and pain equipments for chronic pill popping kinksters and fetishers.

'Oh fuck! What's this shit?' Gouda lets out a loud whistle inspecting the equipments.

'So, this is where the bigrolling kinksters set and enjoy live action! Well, atleast he was having a jolly good time! I have always imagined what it would be like to be invited to such a party—I mean I am not like that, boss—just that I am curious.'

'You are too late, Gouda. Party season is clearly over.'

'Clearly—but this place is something else…and that horrid smell—what the fuck is it?'

Its a nasty river-bottom smell, of ash and fish bones, a foul smell of decay and all things breaking down. The table starts swaying in front of Silva's eyes like some special effect, a slow swelling and ebbing, and he knows his eyes are releasing water from the smell of chemicals in the room. A dull thud makes Silva freeze.

'You heard that?'

'What?'

'Shhhhh listen.'

'There it is again.'

A faint 'thud' repeated at constant intervals. The men move with disbelieving silence towards the sound which seems to come from the darkest part of the room. There is a squelching sound and

Gouda steps back. He has stepped on something.

'What the fuck—'

It is Valentine butting his head against the soundproof wall again and again like a lunatic.

'Fuck! Is he alive?'

'Help me lift him—'

The almost lifeless body has half its face to the wall. The men try not to breathe in the sour nauseating smell, the smell of everything organic breaking down.

'Uughh filthy shit-like smell!' Gouda swears.

The comatose eyes seem to be staring at nothing more than an imaginary point in space with as much life as an empty cocoon. Silva wraps his hands strongly around the body's limp waist and lifts him up. He is as light as paper. Greasy mass of grey wisps cling to his skull, his countenance is that of a wax sculpture.

'Looks like he had some kind of seizure. Shit the stink—'

Silva is already on the phone relaying information on the development.

His skin is yellow and reeking, there are dark purple shadows under his eyes. But the real shock is how much of his hair has fallen out.

'The ambulance should be here soon—what is this?' Silva extends his finger and scraps off a tiny yellow pea shaped residue near the inner corner of Valentine's eye and holding it at a sufficient distance sniffs delicately. He knows the smell to well. He is peering inside his eyes, when Valentine's body goes into a seizure all the way from his neck to his toes, his white lips clamped together and his fingers clawing at nothing. Then it stops and his hands lay limp.

'The ambulance will be here soon, but do you think he will make it?'

'For some time, at least.'

It is then that Silva notices the picture scrunched in Valentine's fist. He opens the actor's fingers and places the photograph on his left palm and irons out the wrinkles with the flat of the right palm. It is not difficult to recognize the man in the picture. He has seen him before. It is the same man whose picture he has seen in Este's house. The man she had introduced as her uncle. But that's not the only thing Silva recalls. He knows he has seen Este's mysterious uncle somewhere else, at Valentine's chamber, the shy assistant who was too nervous to look at him.

'Fool! Bloody fool!' A slow fire crackles in his throat. Silva hunches his shoulders and leans against the wall. He is shaking. The air around him is filled with muffled sounds of ambulance and police sirens.

'Bloody fool,' he keeps muttering to himself as he steps out into the night.

43

Dorab Silva
Monday, 23 November
The Dune, Este's house
Case no. 55/63/2018/dineshthackray/

Dorab Silva's wife often told him that there was something unfair about the brute truth. You cannot win against it. It does not give you a chance to swing in or out of the cracks. Did she want him to stay in the grey? Did she doubt that he would be able to handle the bruteness of the truth?

Did Este also see through the cracks?

Was he so obvious?

The whore saw through you from day one.

The dying light coming in from the sky is slowly sucked into the increasingly inky interiors of the moving car. Silva turns up the news broadcast on the radio, but does not listen to a single word. His state is not different from a man blinded by turn of events, now trying to re-manoeuvre his way back into consequence. He is ashamed of the fact that he wants nothing more than to fuck the whore with his hands around her throat. His motives make him uncomfortable.

You sucker—you gullible fool—

Did the drifter in him need the whore so badly that he had failed to see the signs? Maybe lots of sex does drown a lot of pain and most of common sense. When his soft knock on Este's door goes unanswered, the sharp kick does the job. Silva let himself in quietly because he can hear her voice. For a second, he cannot make sense of the shapes intertwined in the dark, locked in the familiar rhythmic movements. She is fucking a man with a monstrous back. He watches them transfixed as hot anger washes down his tense body like boiling wax. Silva switches on the lights and realizes it is not Este.

The man with the fleshy back and a bulky head jerks up, his angry curse dim to throaty gurgles when he sees the gun attached to the officer's belt. The girl is pretty and dark and long-limbed and the chain around her neck says 'Lil Lillette'.

'Where is Este?' Silva asks.

'Este? She is gone! With her baby. I bought this place from her. Paid good money—she may not be coming back and I always fancied this—'

'Gone? Where—'

'No idea. She left a few days ago—was it a week ago—can't say for sure. She didn't say where she was going and to whom. Her uncle though is still here, in the other room—'

'Her uncle is here? In her room?'

'Strange man, strange name. Been locked inside for several days. Has he done something wrong? I like to keep out of trouble—' Lil Lillette tries to keep fear from creeping into her voice.

'Which way?' Silva asks.

The room resembles a third-rate whore salon with its red and blue tiles. He is lying there on the tiles his pallor of mixed hues of death. Lying still like a pile of used clothing. Not trying to hide or just sleeping, one would think.

Silva closes the door behind him. With a careful movement, he stretches out the white-faced corpse on the wooden planks of the floor. The dead man's extremities are criss-crossed with dehydration in a way that reminds him of the wind patterns on a map. Two large inverted swirls made caves out of his pulled taut cheeks which peak at very high cheekbones, a pair of deep whorls on either side of his nostrils lends an almost prideful definition to the dead man's nose. The lips have turned blue and the gazeless eyes are like green marbles with a thick rind of darkness around the edge of the iris and clusters of yellow pearls. Did Este realize he was getting close to the truth. Poisoned him, even if not enough to kill him? All the while when he was having sex with her it was she who was actually fucking him?

Silva sits down heavily on the bed as the faces of Valentine, Akhouri, Hiri and Este flash before his eyes. Este had blind-sided him. And now she is gone. Lost to him with her mysteries intact. He feels weak and spent.

It is always a brutal moment when a man comes to face his failure and apprehends his life as a man of flesh, possessed of frailty, stares at a bleak past and an uncertain future.

44

Rathi and Este
Sometime in the present
The Dune harbour

Roobi Bloo looks drained in the morning light, its contours blurred like an old whore's. All night there'd been a great deal of rain and the moist grey sky splits with lightning and thunder. Rathi washes her face with icy cold water and pats her cheeks to get some life into them. She cannot do much about the bloodshot eyes but for the first time in days she feels her strength return since her 'accident'. A long-sleeved shirt, a warm camisole and her car keys are all she needs. A waitress with a capsized face takes Rathi's order. When the drink arrives it is too sweet but the saccharin shock feels good. She touches the glass's cold rim with her lips feeling the smooth frost against her skin and swallows another sip like a nervous bird dipping its beak in a pearly liquid. Silhouetted against the foggy window is Este. Her face remains inscrutable as she crosses two rows to sit next to her.

'We are Family'—Rathi had refused to acknowledge Este's damning words the last time they were together.

'Cold day,' Este remarks. Rathi nods. Both of them have the expression of those who don't know what to do with the truth now that its splayed in front of them. From outside somewhere came the shrill whistle of a trawler, a raucous shotgun blast on a rainy day.

'Missy, I would not judge Mister—your pop—so bad...' Este says without meeting her eyes.

'He never hit me, treated me better than my own mar'm, I forgave him long back...' Este said. 'Missy, you are no sister of mine. Will never be. Neither was your pop my pop.... not in the normal way that is. This girl here—she ain't your sister. She is nothing to you but she is my world. If Mister wasn't there I wouldn't have her. So, I have nothing to complain about. It's the nature of things now—'

An inexplicable sense of finality descends with Este's words.
It is the nature of things now.

Rathi is astounded that while she feels trapped in despairing emotions, Este seems to have accepted her damnation so easily. A girl had to have seen particularly demented things to remain so indifferent. Her heart lurches when the baby stares at her with her father's eyes.

'How old is she?' Rathi asks if only to break the uncomfortable stillness they are immersed in. Este did not answer and Rathi does not prod any further. The women lapse into a silence of two people joined by circumstances beyond their control. The quiet between the two women was disturbed only by the slurp of the baby and its gummy chewing.

'We are leaving...leaving for good. Just wanted to tell you before we go so you don't come back with pictures and such—I won't be here to save you now,' Este says with a smile which seems to measure the infinite distance between them which can never be bridged.

Este walks out of the bar and beyond the turnstile and into the rapidly crowding trent bridge. Holding the baby protectively, Este doesn't look back. The wind picks up, but Rathi continues to stare in their direction as the mother and child move down the muddy bank. From a distance, she is just about able to make out the passengers boarding a large ship, *The Marine Sail*. The rain takes away all chance of vision and the water is as grey and opaque as a pewter plate. Far away, the bucking masts on some boats sway lazily, their motion arrested by the turn of the wind. Rathi plants her feet apart, thrusts her hands into her pockets and looks out over the white roar of the ocean. Past the junky boats, the screwjacks, the passenger trolleys, the giant ship's greased rollers, past the wooden lighthouse at the spit's far end, past the dark hulks of gigantic ancient trawlers, the ship moved as if towards the clouded mountain…beyond to some mysterious destination.

Rathi feels very tired but she knows she will sleep well tonight after a long time.

45

DAILY NEWS
Update by Molly Limaye | From issue dated Monday, 3 December

> *Valentine seems to have shrunk a size from the time he was extricated in a dishevelled state from his own basement. A police team led by ACP Dorab Silva have been stopped from visiting him. Doctors feel the patient needs time to recover... lots of time—*

Daily News Chief Reporter Molly Limaye's mouth twitches impatiently as she struggles with the medical terminology and legal jargon for her news articles. It's her last day at *Daily News* and she has just finished adding the final touches to her piece. She wants to give it a last-minute go-over before mailing it to the editor before the 8 p.m. deadline.

> *—He will live they say, though they continue to despair about the mixed colours on his face and his chest sticking out like a birdcage, his graying gums and his diminishing skin tone. That, and the fact that he does not have any memory of the sequence of events which led to his virtual entombment. The doctors are relieved he no longer requires the intravenous device feeding liquid food in the plastic bag into the vein or the catheter inserted to catch urine. Valentine doesn't speak much, but his face criss-crosses with agitation if the lights are switched off. During the day he stares upwards with eyes like shutterless bins at an empty sky reflecting the emptiness of his own obliterated memory. Sometimes*

he mumbles words mechanically like a man sentenced to carry out the sentence of death in life. Actress Kimmy White, seen constantly next to Mr Valentine, has vowed not to leave his side till he recovers even if it takes a lifetime. She has been telling the nurses at the hospital that reports of split with Mr Valentine as part of the media's 'overactive imagination'. Fifty-year-old Neville Valentine was rescued from his river facing house-cum-studio in a near dead state several days ago. Authorities have officially determined Mr Valentine's near fatal accident as having been caused by the abuse of prescription drugs. Medical opinion has established beyond doubt that the victim held in captivity was administered sedatives. The police are tight-lipped about the exact condition in which Valentine has been found. Though unconfirmed reports hint at overuse of drugs in a confinement play gone wrong. Valentine's chief medical examiner and president of the Medici Paramedics Association, Dr Diaz has released a statement reproduced below in its entirety.

Dr Diaz, Chief Medical Examiner & President of Medici Paramedics Association

'Mr Neville Valentine is being treated for acute and lethal level intoxication brought about by a suspected combined effect of remote drugs. His breathing presumably got slower and slower, and if he hadn't been rescued in time he would have reached a level which could have blocked oxygen to his brain and led to coma or irreversible brain damage. We have managed to halt the process but the level of damage is to be yet ascertained.'

Known for his strong stand against prescription drugs, Dr Das, Criminal Forensic Pathologist is hinting at unethical drug prescription. Reproduced below are his expert comments as given to DAILY NEWS:

Dr Das, Criminal Forensic Pathologist

'Mr Valentine's condition could be the case of "sloppy over-prescribing" leading to poly-drug intoxication induced respiratory arrest due to the cocktail of drugs in his body. The law must determine through their investigation on how he managed to get his hands on the drugs.'

Molly's face, which has been sombre, lights up at a thought. Tomorrow is the first day at her new job, at a law firm and she wants to make a good impression. She has decided to change her ambitions to suit fashionable moralities and she grins remembering her editor's gobsmacked face when she put in her papers. Several new press releases have landed in her inbox.

Patent Court

The Comptroller General of Patent and Design has denied patent to Medici on several grounds including its alleged failure to meet stipulations under sections 3(d) and 3(b) of the national patent Law. Section 3(d) restricts patents for already known drugs unless the new claims are superior in terms of efficacy while Section 3(b) bars patents for products that are against public interest and do not demonstrate enhanced efficacy over existing products.

Molly reads the press release wordlessly. She wonders if this would be enough? A company like Medici can never be belly up—its proxy lobbies will see to it. Just as she knows Medici will challenge the Regional Court of Pharma Malpractice's order on its Heal drugs on grounds of it being 'ill-informed' and 'hasty' and a conspiracy to derail the 'progress' of science. The line has been crossed so many times; there are no lines. However, Molly has come to consider conventional progress a misnomer. She has decided to put her faith in the primitive model of justice, a concept scoffed at as outdated even by her 'progressive' colleagues. But there had to be a way to rattle Medici's cage and Molly Limaye hopes her new job at the RCPM as a junior researcher will be helpful.

46

Este and Kaayi
Sometime in the present

The Marine Sail
80 km off the Dune harbour, heading to the eastern coast

'...*and most of all, dear Este, we need to correct the betrayals—but will it be enough?*'

Este re-reads Akhouri's letter with an emotional indifference to her own traumatic history. Swamped by a silence not distinguishable from an alienation of emotion she wonders what went in his mind in the final moments.

Este cannot exactly pinpoint when Akhouri came into her life. What she does remember is that she reacted instinctively to him. That he was a long lost relative trying to trace them for years did not impact her as much as what Akhouri actually presented to her when he inexplicably appeared at her door several month ago; almost a physical ridge for her to cross over into a life less base. Like the other things in her life she accepted his existence and his truths without question. Perhaps they presented to her the possibility of a life other than the pre-ordained. That she has a past which did not begin in a whorehouse. He brought her face to face with the part of her mind which she never knew existed. And the recognition of that divided her life into two biomes—before, and, after Akhouri. She had listened in wonder to Akhouri's tales of his village, its red soil, its forests, its skies and waters. Till she could taste the soft maguey, smell the flowers and feel the sweet waters in her head. Her initial hesitation and distrust melted in front of his rationale and she found herself listening to his tales from their village. He told her of his mother, the medicine woman. About Hiri, her mother. He told her of Hiri and how she would run in the mountains and how she loved to eat the red fish mixed with crispy maguey fruit. She remembers his face softening when he spoke about her mother and she would look away but not before she heard what he had to tell her…her mother—healthy, whole. And she saw how his eyes became dark with rage when he spoke of the poisoned soil and water. But she was content, for she was suddenly more than what they always told her she was. That an unconscious history at play could have governed her reaction to Akhouri cannot be ruled out.

'Will what you know today be enough to keep your child safe? No. I fear not. Because the betrayals will always be too many. But will you not even try? I am filled with a shame so deep and a pain so intense I cannot breathe when I think of the ease with which my brothers accepted the contempt with which our land was treated. I have nothing left—there is no measure of what I have truly lost. I have lost my strength, my hands lie lose, dear child—sickness eats my tissue, my skin, and will claim me soon—'

If Akhouri's promise of retribution appealed to her, the child offered her something more. The change had already started when she gave birth to the child. The child who she had shunned as proof of her damnation, the absence of choice—the child who established itself in her body without her consent. There was a time so dark when she would dream of selling the baby off to one of the brothels. But then her feelings began to change, from anger and resentment to fear, as if she was scared of the change the child would impose. The child had made her want to live, to move beyond the havoc of her past. Akhouri had explained to her that Kaayi was to be her salvation, a new chance.

'My mother did not do what was demanded of her. And so the whole machinery devoted itself to the destruction of her difference. They beat her spirit and then her body till she died.

When your days are good you will be tempted to forget what happened. And get on with your life—and then it will happen again. So, never forget. But the choice will be yours—'

And Este had chosen. With a subjectless gaze, Este surveys the approaching landscape. The muggy, smutchy look is gone and the sky is almost a decisive cobalt blue. The baby farts softly and nuzzles into her warm breast. She knows she is forever and inextricably tied to the child's yet unformed fate. Just as the child's fate is linked to the land.

Sometime in the future

Rangi, (150 km off the Dune's eastern coast)

Legend has it that old maguey trees have been around for thousands of years. The unbroken line of giant grey-green boab maguey trees reach into the clouds and beyond. Native to the eastern mountains of the Dune, the tree grows upside down, with its roots in the air and its trunk buried in the ground. They say it has mythical properties. For many tribes in the region it acts as a signpost and as a guide for travellers, also plays an important role in the ecosystem of the area, providing fruit, water and medicine. And as befitting a legend, they are monumental in proportions reaching heights of hundreds of feet and trunks of diameters upto 36 feet. Because these trees never form rings in their barks with growth, their age can't be determined. They are said to house the most powerful spirits of healing. The boab maguey is the richest fruit of the Dune. Even children know its smell, the flavour of its outer shell and its inner meat. And on dark rainy days it's particularly intoxicating, suited for big feasts for hungry gods.

The settlers around the forests often see a little girl who spends a lot of time exploring the musky damp woods which is exploding with unknown herbs and mysterious yellow flowers of multiple fragrances. The little girl's eyes are blue with gold specks and she smiles without reason.

Epilogue

Brand Ambassadors are everywhere because they work. They take the multi-million dollar corporations and put a human face on them. They are the smile, handshake, helpful answer, and compliment the consumers remember when they think of the brand in return.

Central Consumer Protection Council (CPCC) has discussed the issue of celebrity endorsement. There are proposed revisions to advertising laws which will require celebrities to use products before endorsing them. Celebrities, for the most part, do not endorse products they believe in. They endorse products that pay them the right price. Are brand ambassador truly unaware of the long and complicated history of products they endorse, such as— faulty brake lines of cars, allergic reactions of balms, cancer causing whitening skin creams, or body disrupting energy drinks, antibiotic-laced honey, or sugar stoked soft drinks, tobacco and liquour and medicines? Do brand ambassadors share the questionable nutritional benefits of the products they endorse? If faced by facts which point at questionable nutritional benefits will they share the same with the public? Or end their endorsement with them? Celebrities claim that brand ambassadors cannot be held liable for everything they are associated with. They say that while they don't want to be associated with, what might possibly be perceived, as a bad product—but how can they be responsible for vetting, researching, and confirming that every brand and every product they associate with is a 100 per cent safe, healthy and true to its promise? Isn't that the responsibility of the government bodies that give manufacturing licences, retail permissions and health and safety certificates to the companies that create these products for the market?

Jesse Torres,
Business Expert

We are all supplies.
The sooner we get that the better.

—Anonymous